"This is Paddington, honey . . .

a working man's neighborhood. This rug we're sitting on set you back at least three thousand pounds and there's another five thousand in rags in your closet. Now you've either got a secret admirer or you're a very top-dollar hooker. Which is it?"

She tried for indignation but couldn't make it. Instead she started sputtering and attempted to free her wrists from the vise of Carter's grasp.

He squeezed hard, and then harder.

"Jesus," she cried, "I should call the coppers . . ."

"I already have," Carter growled. "My name is Carter. Nick Carter. Ring a bell?"

NICK CARTER IS IT!

"Nick Carter out-Bonds James Bond."

—*Buffalo Evening News*

"Nick Carter is America's #1 espionage agent."

—*Variety*

"Nick Carter is razor-sharp suspense."

—*King Features*

"Nick Carter is extraordinarily big."

—*Bestsellers*

"Nick Carter has attracted an army of addicted readers . . . the books are fast, have plenty of action and just the right degree of sex . . . Nick Carter is the American James Bond, suave, sophisticated, a killer with both the ladies and the enemy."

—*The New York Times*

FROM THE NICK CARTER KILLMASTER SERIES

THE ALGARVE AFFAIR
THE BUDAPEST RUN
CARIBBEAN COUP
THE DEATH DEALER
THE DEATH STAR AFFAIR
THE DECOY HIT
THE DUBROVNIK MASSACRE
EARTHFIRE NORTH
THE GOLDEN BULL
THE GREEK SUMMIT
HIDE AND GO DIE
THE HUMAN TIME BOMB
THE ISTANBUL DECISION
THE LAST SAMURAI
NORWEGIAN TYPHOON
OPERATION SHARKBITE
THE PARISIAN AFFAIR
THE REDOLMO AFFAIR
REICH FOUR
RETREAT FOR DEATH
THE SATAN TRAP
SIGN OF THE COBRA
THE SNAKE FLAG CONSPIRACY
SOLAR MENACE
THE STRONTIUM CODE
THE SUICIDE SEAT
TIME CLOCK OF DEATH
TRIPLE CROSS
TURKISH BLOODBATH
WAR FROM THE CLOUDS
THE YUKON TARGET
ZERO-HOUR STRIKE FORCE

NICK CARTER

KILLMASTER

OPERATION SHARKBITE

CHARTER BOOKS, NEW YORK

OPERATION SHARKBITE

A Charter Book/published by arrangement with
The Condé Nast Publications, Inc.

PRINTING HISTORY
Charter Original/April 1984

ISBN: 0-441-63424-9

Charter Books are published by The Berkley Publishing Group,
200 Madison Avenue, New York, N.Y. 10016
PRINTED IN THE UNITED STATES OF AMERICA

Dedicated to the men of the Secret Services of the United States of America

ONE

Nick Carter slipped binoculars from a leather case at his side and stretched out prone on the top of the ridge. To his left was the sea, pounding angrily against the rocky cliffs. Now and then a patch of fog would drift inland, bringing a chill dampness with its gray, enveloping fingers.

Behind him, about five miles back, were the lights of Cardiff, Wales. They gleamed eerily in the misty night sky. Directly in front of him, three hundred yards across a deep gorge bit into the cliffs by the millennia of angry seas and unforgiving winds, was another cliff.

Below him, in the belly of the gorge, was Grayburn House.

The binoculars were specially fitted with night lenses. Through them Carter could see clearly the winding road that led down from the inland side of the gorge. A Rolls-Royce, using only its parking lights, snaked down the road.

Carter tracked it, his eyes straining at the blacked-out windows.

He could see nothing, no one beyond the tinted glass, inside the smoothly creeping machine.

A massive electronic gate swung quietly open, and the rich man's land yacht rolled through.

Carter cursed when the car didn't stop at the mansion's looming oak doors. Instead it moved on around to the side of the house where what were once stables had been converted into a large multicar garage.

There would be no chance now to get a look at the VIP who would soon step out of the Rolls and enter Grayburn House.

At least, not yet.

The house itself was not huge by Welsh country mansion standards. It was Victorian in style, with two front stories that fed into a third in the rear, where the land inclined toward the sea.

Carter spotted three watchers: one in the front, at the gate; another at the seawall in the rear; and a third patrolling the roof, left to right, front to back, in a steady military pace.

The AXE Killmaster smiled to himself.

Old Lord Grayburn—peer of the realm, upholder of the dignity of King and Country—would roll over in his tomb if he knew how his daughter was using her inheritance and his house.

They called themselves JOUST. It stood for nothing, really; it was no more than a code name.

It had started out years before as nothing more than a right-wing club made up of ultraconservatives. They met twice a year in London or Paris or New York to rail against the Red Menace and throw their support behind any anti-Communist group that tickled their fancy.

But then, about a year ago, the complexion of JOUST began to change radically.

They lost their zeal for exposure and quietly slid underground. What little did leak out was military in nature. What had been just talk of the Red Menace now turned to real saber rattling.

Men of talk became men of action.

Their motto became "Strike first and strike hard."

Eventually these different rumblings reached ears in Washington, London, and Moscow.

JOUST had begun to go military.

High-ranking American and British Army and Navy officers had been approached to join their ranks. How many had actually been recruited was unknown.

Moscow became alarmed before anyone else when one

of the diplomats in Algiers had been kidnapped and, soon after, assassinated.

At first, wild-eyed free-lance terrorists had been blamed.

But slowly, through the worldwide underground, that theory had evaporated and JOUST had surfaced.

This was the first incident. There were others, less serious, but nevertheless potent enough to sting the Big Bear's backside into action.

Anton Brilovitch, a top KGB fieldman, was dispatched to London. His orders: infiltrate JOUST; if possible, find the organization's top man; and terminate.

Instead, Brilovitch himself had bought the farm.

To add insult to injury, his mutilated remains had been crated up and shipped to the Russian embassy in London as "Television Equipment."

That brought MI5 on the scene.

JOUST became the personal baby of agent Harry Lords. It was decided that he would allow himself to be turned and become the inside man.

An outside man would also be necessary, and since Washington had also gotten edgy enough about JOUST by now, they asked if they could supply the second team member.

MI5 agreed, on one condition: Harry Lords got to pick his own helpmate.

There was no question in the Englishman's mind.

He had worked with Nick Carter on three very dangerous and tricky assignments in the past. If he was going to expose his ass, he wanted an experienced man like Carter to cover it.

Lords also knew that Carter was connected in Washington with a top, supersecret agency. He didn't know the agency, but he did know of its existence and that, through it, Carter had a license to kill if necessary.

Nick Carter was his man.

So for the past five months, Carter had been Harry Lords's only backup and link to the world outside JOUST.

How had Lords gotten in?

Lenore Grayburn.

She had made the first overture toward his recruitment at a fashionable West End party.

Lords had carried it several steps further in the master bedroom suite of Lenore Grayburn's town house in London.

Besides believing passionately in rightist causes, Queen, and Country, and despising the Soviet threat, Lady Grayburn delved deeply into the joys of the flesh.

In six months, Harry Lords had done his job well. He was almost completely integrated into the upper echelons of JOUST. Tonight would be the crowning moment.

Tonight Lords would meet the top man himself, the man who had turned JOUST militant. Also, Lenore Grayburn had hinted that the final solution to the Communist problem had been on the drawing boards for months. Soon that final solution would be put into effect, and Lords was to be a major part of it.

It was time to make the kill, quietly and discreetly.

Harry Lords was on the inside.

Nick Carter was on the outside.

London and Washington—as well as Lords and Carter—hoped that this would be a quiet evening.

Lords would get the intelligence they wanted, get out, and tomorrow morning, MI5 in the U.K. and the FBI in the States would swoop down and do the collecting.

But in case things didn't go smoothly, Killmaster N3 had come prepared.

Wilhelmina, his 9mm Luger, was leathered under his left armpit. She had been fitted with a special silencer that suppressed all flash as well as sound. Hugo, Carter's quiet, death-dealing stiletto, was in its spring-loaded chamois sheath on his right forearm, and Pierre, the tiny gas bomb, was between his legs, playing third testicle.

For extra firepower, a Beretta 9mm Model 4 sub lay along Carter's side. It was a sweet little weapon, with a 550-round-per-minute cyclic rate for good accuracy close up or at a distance. The double—fore and aft—trigger device allowed firing on semi-auto or full auto mode without messing with levers.

If that wasn't enough, Carter carried four M-34 fragmentary grenades and sulfurous flash balls in a small web pouch attached to his belt in the small of his back.

The beeper on Carter's belt sounded a couple of short ones.

So far so good. Everything progressing A-OK.

It was activated by a small sending device strapped to Harry Lords's left leg.

This was the third time Lords had pressed the device since the vigil had started at around ten o'clock. Two or three short beeps just to let Carter know that everything was cool on the inside.

It was just past one in the morning now.

The minutes dragged by. Carter's psyche hungered for a cigarette, but he didn't dare. The firefly glow at the end of a butt could be seen, even in this grayness, one hell of a lot farther than the distance from him to the sentry on the roof.

More lights popped on in the mansion's top-story windows. Again Carter brought the binoculars to his eyes. He could see movement in the huge room, but he couldn't distinguish faces through the sheer curtains.

More waiting.

A little sweat gathered in the small of his back even though the air was almost chill.

His watch read 1:50.

There was movement at the far corner of the house. Carter swerved the glasses.

It was the rear end of the Rolls. The big car backed smoothly around and made for the front steps. Once there, it rocked gently and the passenger side rear door swung open.

One of the big oak doors opened and Lady Lenore Grayburn stepped out.

Carter smiled as he cased her from four-inch heels to glossy, jet black mane.

The lady, dressed in a silky, sleeveless, clinging sheath, was all curves in and out, with a lot of top and just the right amount of bottom. Her face was regal and haughty, but nonetheless beautiful in the rather somber English way.

She talked to someone hidden just beyond the door, nodded a few times, and then moved her long legs down to the Rolls.

Just as she ducked her head to enter the car, a hand and arm came up to help her in.

Electricity traveled from Carter's toes clear up to curl the short hairs on the back of his neck.

On the end of the dark sleeve was gold braid. A lot of it. Carter tried to count the gold stripes; one large, and. . . .

The movement was too swift, barely a blink, making it impossible to catch the number of smaller gold circles.

But it still said worlds.

The uniform was Navy, and the rank was admiral. Because Carter hadn't caught the uppermost gold stripe, it was impossible to tell if its owner was British or American. Because he hadn't been able to count the smaller stripes, he didn't know how far above rear admiral the officer was.

But it was a start, if needed.

Hopefully it wouldn't be. If all had gone well, Harry Lords now knew the big man's name and the big operation he had masterminded.

"This is the final coup," Lady Grayburn had confided to Lords. "The one slap in the face the Russians can't ignore!"

The Rolls glided away from the front stoop toward the open gates. As it went through, the sentry—in civvies—snapped to attention and executed a very military salute.

The big machine was halfway up the winding drive toward the inland end of the gorge and the main north-south road when the communicator on Carter's belt beeped again, once. . . .

Twice.

And then began a steady hum.

That was it, the alternate signal. The send unit on Lords's leg had a hold catch on the button. A couple or three quick beeps meant everything was okay.

Pushing the button all the way in, locking it on hold, meant trouble. Big trouble.

Come get me!

Adrenaline poured through Carter's body. Instantly, he was up and running in a combat crouch. He had already reconnoitered the cliffside for a way down if needed.

And, God knew, he needed it now. Harry Lords wasn't the kind of agent who shouted fire when there was only smoke.

Carter found the path in seconds and, like a black cat, moved down through rocks, undergrowth, and scrub trees. There was an eight-foot fence at the base of the gorge, surrounding the complete perimeter of the property in a horseshoe, its open mouth facing the sea.

The only way in, unless you flew or swam, was through the front gate. It was still open after letting the Rolls through, and Carter headed for it.

He had already killed the beeper. There was no more need for it. The call had come and Carter was answering it.

As he moved, he primed the Beretta's chamber with a slug from the feeder, and jammed the retracting handle forward to release the safety and make the weapon ready for firing. With the lanyard over his left shoulder, he adjusted the sub along his back from left shoulder blade to right hip. A twist of the body and a roll of the arm would bring the sub's muzzle up in a second to spew death.

A grove of poplars started along the fence line about twenty yards seaward of the gate. Carter stayed deep in those until he was up the lane and in front of the gate at a ninety-degree angle out about twenty-five yards.

The sentry was making notations on a clipboard as Carter unsheathed Wilhelmina and dropped to one knee. In first firing position, he rested his left elbow against a tree and extended his forearm across his sight line. Then he brought the Luger's extended snout up in his right hand and rested it across his left wrist.

One glance up at the skyline told Carter that the sentry on the roof was on the backside of his patrol.

Take a deep breath, release, squeeze off between pulse beats.

Phffi . . . and then a second, just in case.

It wasn't needed.

The first hollow-point caught the man dead center in the chest, carrying the bones of his sternum away and out through a fist-sized hole in the middle of his back.

The second slug was higher and slightly to the left, probably near his heart. But the guy was already dead.

The spreading lead had thrown him up against the small guardhouse. He was slipping down, leaving his gore on the whitewashed wood, when Carter caught him.

Five seconds later he was sitting on a stool in the guardhouse, his dead eyes gazing at nothing, the Sten propped across his chest.

Carter did another quick check of the roof and an eyeball of the vast lawn and front gardens.

Nothing. No one. Just a slight breeze ruffling the leaves of three oaks halfway between Carter and the house.

He made for them in a dead-out sprint.

From the shadows of the trees Carter got a good look at the garage.

An older model Jag roadster, a huge Daimler, and a Bentley took up three of eight stalls behind the open doors.

A guard sat in a chair just in front. He was rocking back and forth, tapping the back of the chair against a post. A cigarette drooped from one corner of his mouth, and a Sten gun lay across his knees.

Carter scowled.

From this distance he could drop him with the silenced Luger, just as he had done the gate guard. But the man's chair was sitting on a cement apron. If Carter got him with a slug, there was a good chance the Sten and the chair would make one hell of a racket coming down.

Enough for the guard on the roof or one inside the house to hear?

Carter guessed yes.

A low stone fence at the end of the garage led down to the formal gardens and more trees.

Carter knew the deadly technique of killing a man silently. It was only a tiny piece of his extensive training.

He holstered Wilhelmina and searched the ground around his feet until he found a stone.

Still in a crouch, he heaved the stone toward the wall. It hit once and then skittered down the path.

The guard came to his feet, bringing the Sten up. He searched the darkness with furrowed brows, but it looked as though he was going to remain in place.

Carter filled his hand again and tossed another stone, hoping that the man wouldn't see the trajectory against the gray sky.

He didn't, and moved off in search of the disturbance.

When he hit the line of trees, Carter himself moved out. He crab-walked parallel to the guard, keeping the trees between them. Carter couldn't see him, but he could hear the crunch of his boots on the gravel path.

When the man stopped, Carter kept going and then angled left, reaching the inner edge of the trees about five yards behind the man.

Carter tensed the muscles of his right forearm, and the tiny spring in Hugo's sheath activated. The hilt filled the palm of his hand, and he coiled his legs in readiness.

The guard was bent over, examining the path near the wall. Then he straightened and took a look over the wall.

Just at that moment, a rabbit skittered from the trees and went hell-bent along the path toward the house.

Carter shook his head in wonderment. Luck was with him tonight.

He hoped it was with Harry Lords as well.

The guard chuckled, muttered something under his breath that Carter didn't catch, and relaxed his hold on the Sten.

He started back toward the house, and Carter, silent as a

stalking animal, moved behind him.

When Carter was pretty sure the point of attack would send the Sten sailing into soft ground instead of noisy gravel, he made his move.

He was on the guard in a split second, his left arm coming up the other man's front, knocking his arms into the air. The Sten sailed, and Carter kept his arm going.

He pinned the guard's arm in with his shoulder under the armpit and jammed the inner part of his elbow between his teeth to cut off any cry. At the same time, Carter's right hand was darting upward like lightning beneath the man's chin.

The point of the stiletto went into the guard's throat at the jugular.

He was dead in Carter's arms before Hugo's tip found his brain.

Without even stopping the thrust of his movement, Carter rolled the body into the trees. The Sten quickly joined the body, and Carter was on a dead run toward the house.

Inside the garage was a single door leading to a hallway. The hallway ended in another door that apparently opened into the middle story. Just before the second door there were two sets of narrow stairs, one going up, one going down.

Carter chose up, and took them three at a time.

At the top there was a long hall with doors on both sides. At the end of the hall was a large window. Carter figured it looked down at the patio, the pool, the seawall, and the sea beyond.

A tall, rangy guy in khaki and a black beret with a standard issue .45 on his hip stood gazing intently out the window.

Carter was halfway down the hall, Wilhelmina extended in his right hand, when the guy became aware of the intruder's presence.

He started his turn slowly, an odd, leering grin on his face. When he saw that Carter wasn't one of his comrades, he flinched and reacted fast, his right hand clawing at the butt of the .45.

His mouth was a perfect O. Carter used it as a target and sent a slug from Wilhelmina through the roof of his mouth into his brain.

He caved in like a felled oak, and Carter stepped over his body to the window without a pause.

"Son of a bitch," he growled when he realized what the rangy guy had been watching.

Walking around the pool toward the seawall was Harry Lords. He was barefoot and stripped to the waist. Even from a distance Carter could see that the British agent's face and body had been worked over.

But what drew his concentration most was the fact that the man's hands were tied behind his back and there was a blindfold over his eyes.

"Good God," Carter breathed.

There was little doubt of it.

The eight, black-bereted men escorting Harry Lords made up a firing squad.

It was to be an execution.

TWO

Carter took the situation and the perimeter in at a glance.

They were guiding Lords toward the low stone wall that fronted the sea. He was flanked by two men with lone .45s on their hips. The firing squad followed in single file: six khaki-clad men carrying M-1 carbines.

Crazy, Carter thought. *These nuts actually think that they're an army!*

The window before him was sealed. Moving to his side he could see balconies jutting from what he hoped were French doors or windows that would open into the rooms off the hall to his right and left.

Below the right balcony was a flat-roofed gazebo he might make without breaking a leg in the jump.

He chose that one, then tried the door.

Locked.

He stepped back, aimed, and splintered the jamb with the heel of his right boot. He followed his foot into the room and scanned with Wilhelmina.

Empty.

The Luger disappeared under his left arm, and he brought the Beretta sub around into the action.

The French doors opened easily. Carter stepped out onto the balcony and dropped to one knee at the rail.

They had backed Harry Lords to the wall. His two guides, evidently in command, had moved farther away to his right and left. They also stood with their backs against the wall but were well out of the line of fire. The six-man squad was settling into a firing line.

Carter had precious little time to make much of a choice.

He settled the stationary stock against his shoulder. Sighting through the L-type rear sight, he reached forward and flipped up the sub's specially installed night illumination forward sight, then slid his finger over the forward trigger: semi-auto mode, three-round bursts.

The officer on the right went with the first two bursts, a grouping of six holes no bigger than a fist in the middle of his gut.

He toppled from sight into the sea.

His body had barely made an exit when the night sight found the other officer. This one's reactions were good. The Beretta had scarcely barked, sending his comrade to hell, when he dropped to one knee, a hand clawing for the .45 at his side.

Carter caught him on the way down. Three slugs in the neck nearly took his head from his body.

The six-man squad was in chaos. They whirled in full circles, carbines at the ready, trying to find the source of the sub's chatter.

"Harry!"

"Gotcha!"

"Your left . . . a fountain . . . get your ass behind it!"

Lords dived, skittered, and rolled.

The words had barely left Carter's lips when he moved his finger to the rear, full auto trigger.

He sprayed a figure eight right to left and back again until the Beretta clicked on empty.

Two of the six bought it on the first time across. Their khaki shirts spurted blood as the slugs tore into and through them, sending their bodies flying grotesquely across the cement.

Three others dived for what cover they could find: another fountain, a tree, and the pool itself.

It took a second to eject the old magazine and jam a new forty-round feeder into the Model 4.

The sixth shooter had held his ground and kept his head.

On one knee he was firing at Lords and the fountain. The agent, by sense and feel, had gotten most of his body in cover.

But not all of it.

One, maybe two, of the slugs from the carbine found their mark. Carter couldn't be sure.

He leveled in on the back of the lone man and sent off a full auto burst. The 9mm killers stitched him from his belt to the base of his skull.

His buddy in the pool caught the flash from the Beretta and came up over the side with his M-1. Slugs chipped stone all around Carter, but the squat stone railing let none of them through.

Carter sent one burst into the water and then went over the rail.

It was too fast and too unexpected for all three of them.

When they started firing again at the flying figure, Carter's booted feet had already found the roof of the gazebo.

He gave with the jolt of the fall, curled into a ball until his roll stopped, and ended flat out.

The guy in the pool was no slouch. He had already changed positions, moving into the more shallow end.

Now he was hunkered down, with the concrete lip of the pool giving him good cover. Carter could see the muzzle of the M-1, a bit of head, and a small piece of shoulder.

It was not enough for a good shot, even though Carter gave it a try with two short bursts. The slugs raised hell with the water around the man but did no damage.

The others—one behind a large, water-spouting stone cupid and the other protected by an oak tree—were pinning Carter down with constant fire.

If that wasn't enough, someone in the house had gotten the message; all hell had busted loose in the courtyard.

The pool lights went off, and a bare second later two slugs ripped into the shingled roof inches from Carter's left side.

He rolled, swinging his eyes and the Beretta up.

Two of them, dimly outlined, stood on the balcony Carter had so recently vacated. One was leveling a Sten, trying to find Carter's dark-clad body where it merged with the roof. The other was doing the same with a .45.

There was no time for aim.

Carter pressed the rear trigger and kept it pressed, filling the whole balcony with steel-jacketed death.

Where he hit the two, Carter would never know. But hit them he must have.

They disappeared amid screams of pain, shattered glass, and chips of stone.

Again lead whined all around Carter from the three below. The main shooter was the guy in the pool. He was coming from a lower point than the others and therefore coming a lot closer.

Too close.

He had begun a methodical pounding of the thin roof from the underside. Shingles were flying up into the air all around Carter.

It would be only a matter of time before one nailed him.

And how many more JOUST troops were in the house trying to locate his position?

"Harry!" Carter cried, reaching into the pouch at the small of his back and extracting one of the M-34s.

"Yeah!"

"You okay?"

"Halfway," came the agent's strained reply.

"Hit?"

"Yeah."

"Duck farther!" Carter cried, lofting the grenade into the air toward the pool.

He had held it for two seconds before throwing, then ducked his head to count.

One-thousand-one . . . two . . . three . . . four . . . five . . .

The night exploded.

A geyser of water, with the shooter's mangled body at its top, shot straight into the air. A big chunk of the pool's side and bottom was ripped away, and the water was quickly disappearing.

Carter rolled off the gazebo's roof and landed running. He hugged the rear of the house and didn't stop until he reached the corner, near the big oak. The guy behind it had "astounded" written all over his face, right up to the time Carter ripped half of it away with the Baretta.

Carter moved in behind the tree. From this position he had clear shooting on all sides of the spitting cupid.

The last man was there, his eyes wide as they stared at death in Carter's.

"I'm out of ammo."

He slid the M-1 away from him. The clatter it made on the cement was eerie after the thunder that had just taken place in the courtyard.

Carter moved out from behind the oak. He kept the Beretta's muzzle on the guy's gut as he watched him lean forward in the spread position.

Carter moved around the fountain and up toward where the man stood, feet wide, hands resting on the side of the fountain.

"How many in the house?" Carter barked.

"No more. We're it."

"Who was the gold braid who left in the Rolls?"

"Number One."

"I guessed that," Carter spat. "What's his name?"

"I don't know—"

"Bullshit!"

Carter sank a half inch of the Beretta's nose into the soft spot behind the other man's right ear.

"It's true, I swear it! He's Number One. The woman is Number Two. We're all numbers . . . no one knows anybody else's name."

"What was the meeting about tonight?"

"To interrogate your friend."

"And that's all?" Carter hissed. "I don't think so."

The man shrugged.

Carter found the leather thong at his back pocket with his left hand and tugged.

"Know what this is?" he asked, tapping the man's shoulder just enough to be painful.

"Cotch."

"Yeah. In Brooklyn we call it a sap. Know how your head's built? . . . Your brain is a very delicate hunk of meat suspended inside your skull—"

"What the hell do you get beatin' my brains out?" the man cried.

"Didn't say that," Carter replied, his voice low and hard. "Just the right pop jars the brain against the skull's bone structure. Makes you black out. If the tap is a little *too* hard and bruises the brain, you get a concussion."

Sweat was beginning to break out on the back of the man's neck.

"A bruise on your brain meat leaves a scar. If it's reopened by another . . . and another . . . you may die. But if it's done right—by an expert—you just go blind or you're paralyzed for life." Carter lightly tapped the back of the man's head with the sap. "Believe it, laddie, I'm an expert with this."

The movement was clean: a roll into a crouch and a sidestep.

Carter recognized the knife in the guy's right hand as its ugly, curved blade hurtled up toward his belly. It was an Asian curee blade, popular with guerrillas in Southeast Asia.

He sidestepped the thrust and backed off two steps, again leveling the deadly Beretta.

"Drop it!"

"Screw you!"

Carter caught him, chest high, midway in his second lunge. The slugs lifted him until the back of his knees hit the edge of the fountain. His own momentum did the rest.

Seconds after he hit, the bubbling water was a bright red.

Carter sprinted around what was left of the pool to the fountain that had provided cover for Harry Lords.

Correction. Partial cover.

He had taken two slugs. The one in the thigh he could have survived. The other, in his gut . . . no way.

It was a rotten, painful way to get it, but Harry Lords hadn't even squeaked.

"You okay?" Carter had asked.

"Halfway," Lords had replied.

But that last half had run out.

He lay on his side, his right arm extended, the fingers pointing. The hand and fingers of Lords's right hand were crimson with drying blood.

And then Carter saw why.

"Jesus," he gasped, dropping to his knee beside the dead agent and fishing a penlight from his pocket.

There, in the gray-white concrete, were Harry Lords's last words, written by his own hand, in his own blood:

LEAK–BRIDGIT

SHARKBITE
140–40

#1 AD

Carter had a pretty good idea what the #1 AD meant. He'd already gotten a bit of that out of the one by the fountain. The #1 referred to the gold braid he'd seen in the Rolls. The AD, ten-to-one, was Admiral.

Lords hadn't been able to finish the word and add the name.

And it came last.

Obviously, Lords had thought the first two parts were even more important than the identity of Number One.

Carter laid his hand on the dead man's shoulder. "You did good, Harry. I'll figure it out."

Then, suddenly, from somewhere in front of the house an engine roared into life. It was quickly followed by the screaming of tires.

Carter moved, sprinting across the courtyard and through the rear doors. As he ran, he ejected what was left of the Beretta's magazine and jammed in a fresh feeder.

He jacked a shell into the firing chamber just as he crashed through the two huge oak doors.

About twenty yards down the drive toward the gate, the

sporty Jag roadster was lurching along like a butt-shot rabbit.

Whoever the little guy with the glasses and receding hairline was behind the wheel, he was unfamiliar with the Jag's gear box. It looked as though he had missed his upshift out of low and ended up in fourth.

Now the powerful car was straining to get up the rpms to move.

Carter leaped the steps and landed in a dead run toward the back end of the Jag. From this distance he could have wasted the driver with one burst, but he had already lost one foolish prisoner. This one he would like to take.

He could see the man's frightened face in the rearview mirror as he frantically worked at the shift lever. The gears were objecting with teeth-grinding growls, and the big engine was roaring in response to the man's nervous foot.

Carter was five feet from the car when the little man found low. The roar of the engine was deafening now as the car's sloped nose leaped into the air. Tires squealed and the Jag's rounded back end began fishtailing wildly down the drive.

There was nothing to it.

Carter dropped to one knee, found the Beretta's full-auto trigger with his finger, and pumped 9mm shells toward the fleeing car.

They were hitting their mark. He could see dark holes appear on the gray paint.

But the car kept moving.

He lowered the Beretta's muzzle and tried for the tires.

No good.

Even an expert marksman of Carter's caliber couldn't hit the Jag's narrow rubber when the vehicle itself was swerving all over the drive.

The Beretta's firing pin hit on empty just as the car got to the gate.

For a brief second Carter thought he had won anyway.

Going through the gate, the inexperienced driver momentarily lost control, and the Jag started in a slide, its rubber whining wildly. But just when the little man was about to lose it, the left rear fender nicked one side of the gate.

It was just enough.

The car righted and up the gorge it went.

Carter sprinted back to the garage. "Damn!"

The little guy did have brains, and he was thorough.

All four tires on the Daimler and the Bentley were flat.

And then he smelled it. Smoke.

It was coming from the right wing of the house, top floor. Behind the window Carter could see that the drapes and curtains were already alive with flames.

He moved as fast as his now weary legs would take him up the stairs to the top floor.

The room was small, at one time probably no more than a dressing room for the adjoining bedroom.

Through the smoke and the flames, Carter could see an elaborate radio setup. A wastebasket near the curtains still belched fire.

Carter guessed that the wastebasket was the source. Chances were the little rabbit in the Jag was some kind of a radioman. And before he had split, he had dumped whatever records or codes he had into the wastebasket and lit up.

That meant he had been watching the firefight from somewhere in the house. When he realized that the one-man army with the submachine gun was winning, he'd made his play.

Idly, Carter wondered if the little guy had seen his face, either during the fight or afterward, behind the Jag.

If Carter was going on with Lords's gig, he didn't want to be made. Not yet.

The small room was fairly confined and was made more so when Carter closed off the doors. He located two fire extinguishers and then found a hose.

It wouldn't do for the local firefighters to come calling and find the mess in the courtyard.

It took him nearly an hour to get the fire down to embers, and another half hour to jog down the beach and back up the cliffs to where he had left the little Ford.

Fifteen minutes later, Carter was in a phone booth outside an all-night gas station.

"Eight-eight-four-five."

"Code Red," Carter barked. "Third level!"

"Yes, sir."

Ten seconds later a cultured voice came on the line. "Third level here."

"This is Carter. . . . JOUST probe."

"I say, are you the chap teamed up with Lords?"

The guy's voice, to Carter, was maddeningly calm.

"Yeah . . . I was. Harry Lords is dead. Who are you?"

"My God."

"I asked who you were."

"Jarrell . . . Sydney Jarrell, night desk officer, third level."

"What's your clearance?"

"Top."

"Good, get me Hamilton!"

"The commander isn't here. I can reach him—have him call you back. What's your number?"

"Never mind. I'm heading for London now. I'll talk to him there. In the meantime, get some housekeepers down here to tidy up the mess."

"Bodies?"

"Lots. A house in a deep gorge between two cliffs, about five miles north of Cardiff—"

"Grayburn House . . . I know it."

"Okay, get the housekeepers here right away. I think it would be best if everything is calm here before dawn."

"Agreed."

"And have Hamilton get me the name and location of every Navy admiral—American or British—in England."

"I dare say that may take some time . . ."

"It's an hour and fifteen minutes to London. I'll want it when I arrive. And who's Bridgit?"

"Who?"

"I have it from Harry. There was some kind of leak . . . Bridgit."

"In M15?" He sounded insulted.

"You sound like it's never happened before," Carter said dryly. "You do remember—"

"Yes, I do. I'll inform the commander."

"And relay this to the commander. He might make something out of it: SHARKBITE . . . one-forty dash forty."

"What in the world . . . ?"

"I don't know, Sydney, but we'd better find out, and quick. I think it's the key to the pending JOUST operation."

Carter dropped the phone back on its cradle and jogged for the car.

THREE

Lieutenant Calvin Jacobs slipped his hands beneath the wardroom table and dried his sweaty palms on his khaki uniform pants.

His fellow junior and senior officers sat around the wardroom table listening to their skipper, Captain Josh McCoy, regale them with war stories.

Not counting Jacobs, there were eleven officers taking the evening meal aboard the nuclear submarine U.S.S. *Shark*. The eighteen other officers of the *Shark*'s command compliment had gone ashore to eat in the Subic Bay Officer's Club.

They had been at sea, patrolling the China straits and the area around Hunan Island and Hong Kong, for forty-three days.

The ship's crew welcomed a little shore time after so long a period at sea. Portside crew liberty had been granted by the skipper at 1600 hours that afternoon, just one hour after the *Shark* had moved up to Berth Three in the Subic Bay sub base in the Philippines.

Lieutenant Jacobs had gone one step further than the skipper. Surreptitiously, he had granted liberty to nearly half the starboard side of the crew, as well as all the port.

Ship's compliment now at . . . .

Jacobs checked the big round marine clock on the bulkhead over the skipper's shoulder.

Exactly 2000 hours.

There were sixty-two officers and crewmen aboard the *Shark* at thirty minutes before zero hour.

"Your coffee, sir."

Jacobs looked up into the steady blue eyes of Seaman, First Class, Lawrence Clary.

"Thank you, Clary."

Jacobs toyed with his coffee, stirring the heavy mud with a spoon as he watched the wardroom steward move on around the table.

Just before moving through the hatch with his empty tray, Clary turned. Once again his eyes met Jacobs's, and then both of them glanced at the clock.

They nodded and Clary slipped out.

Jacobs knew better than to drink the coffee. It was heavily doped. Already Captain McCoy's voice was beginning to slur as he went on with his rambling tale.

Besides Jacobs and Clary, there were two other members of JOUST among the *Shark*'s crew: the Chief engineer of "R" division, Arthur Redding, and the *Shark*'s nuclear ordnance expert, Lieutenant Commander Ralph Pearson.

Jacobs stood. "Gentlemen, if you'll excuse me . . . I have the watch."

They barely acknowledged his departure.

In ten minutes all of them would be nodding off into a deep sleep.

Harbor traffic command for Subic Bay was one large, all-glass room atop the headquarters building. Inside and out, it was not unlike the traffic control tower for a medium-size airport.

The lights were kept dim so that the operators could better see the green lines and blips on the radar screens before them.

This time of night, with only four destroyers and two subs at berth, there was very little activity in the room. Now and then an operator would answer a weather request from a ship moving in or out of Manila Bay, but beyond that the only talk was of the boredom of the long watch.

It was 2013 hours.

Lieutenant (j. g.) Howard Carlson scanned the bay and sub berths with a pair of night glasses. Even though the air conditioning was turned up high against the tropical heat outside, sweat beaded on the lieutenant's forehead.

"Jesus, Carlson, what the hell are you straining your eyes for? We gonna be invaded or somethin'?"

"No, just the usual."

"Hey, guys," the other man chortled, "Carlson's at it again! I can see the drool comin' out of the side of his mouth. Don't worry, Lieutenant, you'll get your sea duty one of these days!"

Quicker than you think, you dumb bastard, Carlson thought.

Lieutenant (j. g.) Howard Carlson had nothing but contempt for the men he served with at Subic Bay. All of them were peacetime sailors, just putting in their time.

Not Howard Carlson.

He was in the military to fight.

A smile creased his lips as he saw dark shapes materialize in the water fifty yards off the U.S.S. *Shark.*

Soon now, he thought. *Real soon.*

Carlson stood. "Watch my scanners a minute, will you? I've got to make the head."

"Sure."

As he passed the heavy steel security door, Carlson quietly slid its two bolts into the open position.

In the head, he locked the door behind him and rummaged in the center of a large wire wastebasket.

Ten seconds later he slipped a regulation issue gas mask over his head. Once the oxygen canister was checked and adjusted, he went to work on the four screws that held the air conditioning vent into the bulkhead.

When it was off, he again dived into the wastebasket. This time he came up with two canisters labeled "Army Issue—KPG-/201."

A grim smile spread Carlson's lips as he studied the canisters.

They contained a gas that attacked the nerve cells at the base of the brain, rendering the breather unconscious for hours.

He set the canister fuses at five seconds and rolled them into the vent.

The chronometer on his wrist read 2015 hours.

He waited two full minutes, imagining the air around him filling with the odorless, invisible gas.

When he stepped from the head, the two men in black wet suits—Sten guns over their shoulders and gas masks in place—were already pulling the other four men of the watch away from their consoles.

Carlson watched them work until all four men were lying comfortably on the floor in the rear of the room.

"Are they out?"

"Like babies."

"Lock the door!"

Carlson moved to the air conditioning control and reversed the fans. Silently he stood watching the second hand on his chronometer go around three times.

"Okay," he said, pulling the gas mask from his face. "You, take Manila Communications. You, handle the weather!"

"Yes, sir," came the two replies as both dark-suited men pulled off their own masks and slid into swivel chairs.

Carlson moved to the center Harbor Command console and began flipping switches.

"*Shark* and *Blowfin*, this is Harbor Command. Come in, *Shark*."

"*Shark* here, Harbor Command. Beautiful night. What can I do for you?"

"Are you on, *Blowfin*?"

"Aye-aye, Harbor Command."

Carlson wiped the sweat from his forehead and gripped the mike tighter in his hand.

"We're going to have to kill your shore generators for about five minutes, gentlemen. We have to do a power check up here."

"*Blowfin* here. You sure it'll only be a few minutes? Skipper's got a hell of a poker game going on in the wardroom."

"Positive, *Blowfin*," Carlson replied. "Not over ten at the most. No need to crank up your on-board generators. Do you read, *Shark*?"

"Roger, Harbor Command."

Carlson broke the berth-to-shore connection and searched the panel for the right switches.

When he hit them, all ten sub berths disappeared in inky blackness.

Operation Sharkbite was underway.

Jacobs signed the log taking over the watch. He was just sliding his pen back into his pocket when the lights went out.

"Jesus . . . eerie," the duty officer Jacobs had just replaced growled.

"Yeah. Go on down, I've got it."

"Think I'll go up in the tower, get some air. It'll be stifling below in five minutes."

Silently, Jacobs followed him to the ladder that led up to the hatch and conning tower. There was only a faint click as he unsnapped the fold-over of his holster. He lifted the .45 from the leather, then reversed it as the barrel filled his hand.

He waited until the other officer was at the ladder and bathed in the gray night light streaming through the hatch.

The barrel of the .45 caught him just behind the right ear. He slumped against the ladder, and Jacobs caught him before he hit the steel deck.

Using a penlight in his teeth, Jacobs dragged the unconscious man to a gear locker. He put him inside, checked his pulse and breathing, then locked the door.

The intercom was already squawking.

"Officer of the watch, this is the duty chief shoreside gangway."

"Go ahead, Chief."

"What the hell's going on, sir?"

"Harbor Command's running a power check, Chief. No problem, take about ten minutes."

Jacobs guided the penlight down the module until he found the "Engine Room."

"Power, this is Lieutenant Jacobs."

"Aye, sir."

Jacobs knew Chief Engineer Arthur Redding's voice.

"Power up, Chief, but don't switch on the generators yet."

"Aye, sir."

Jacobs again ran his light over the console and switched the intercom to full.

"Attention all hands, attention all hands. This is the duty officer. Harbor is doing a power check. We're running on-board generator for the aft rec area only, repeat, on-board lights in the aft rec area only. All hands below-decks are requested to move to the aft rec area at once."

Jacobs switched off and mounted the ladder to the conning tower. From inside his uniform jacket he produced a pair of night goggles and slipped them over his eyes.

One scan, bow to stern, gave him the count.

Chief and two seamen on the shore gangway.

Two Marine MPs on the dock at the foot of the gangway.

A bow sentry, half awake, moving restlessly over the *Shark*'s long snout.

Two seamen, unloaded carbines on their shoulders, paced the fantail.

All accounted for.

Jacobs shielded the penlight in his hands and flashed it three times toward the murky waters of the bay.

The third flash had barely beamed when twenty men in night goggles and black wet suits poured up pre-set grappling lines to the deck of the *Shark* and the dock beside it.

Lieutenant Commander Ralph Pearson set the oblong black leather case on the desk and released the catch. When the leather lid was pulled up, he stepped back.

"Missile fuse devices, sir . . . four of them, and the arming codes. Commanding officer, Captain Josh McCoy, U.S.S. *Shark*. The skipper sends his compliments."

"Thank you, Commander. Maybe Josh and I can get in

some golf this week. It will take me a few minutes to check these numbers. Want a drink?"

"No, thank you, sir," Pearson replied, standing at ease near the edge of the desk.

Base Commander Captain Rollo Pitts detected the note of disdain in Lieutenant Commander Pearson's voice at the mention of a drink while supposedly still on duty.

Young go-getters, Pitts sighed to himself, *always everything by the book. Oh, well. . . .* He guessed that he himself had once been like that . . . when he was young and fresh out of the Academy. That was back when a battleship had sixteen-inch guns and submarines carried torpedoes.

Now. . . .

Not hiding his distaste for the contents of the leather case, Captain Pitts pulled it across the desk toward him and fished in a drawer for the serial number code books.

"Damn nuisance, checking these little devils in and out every time you hit port."

"Regulations, sir."

"I know that, Commander," Pitts said dryly.

"If we don't get them to you within ten hours of berthing, you'd just have to come and get them."

Pitts nodded and quickly went over the numbers. Pearson made him nervous with his starchiness. He'd be only too happy to get the devices checked in and the gung-ho commander on his way.

If Pearson didn't care for a drink, Captain Pitts did. Officially, he wasn't on duty. It was just such a nuisance that only the base commander could check in the arming devices.

He entered the numbers on a blank form, checked them off, and signed his name.

"If you'll sign the release, Commander?"

"Surely, Captain."

Pearson stepped around the desk. As he took the pen in his left hand, he pulled a silenced Browning from the small of his back with his right.

As he leaned over the desk, he brought the muzzle up against the back of the captain's skull.

The small-caliber slugs were perfect for this type of assassination. Four of them entered Captain Pitts's brain and stayed there without making a mess.

There wasn't even any blood beyond a few drops that stained the back of his collar.

Pearson slipped the gun back under his jacket and caught the body all in one deft movement. Five quick pulls and he dropped the corpse on the washroom floor. He locked the door behind him and transferred the nuclear missile arming devices to a specially rigged harness under his jacket. The empty leather case went into a wastebasket beneath a pile of paper, and the codes found their way into his outside pocket.

He removed the office door key from the captain's ring and palmed it as he stepped into the hall. Shaking his wrist and studying his watch for the two Marine guards at the end of the hall, Pearson locked the door behind his back.

At the elevator he saluted the two guards.

"Captain Pitts asked me to tell you that he doesn't want to be disturbed for at least two hours."

"Yes, sir."

Twenty minutes later, Lieutenant Commander Pearson stepped from the staff car two blocks short of the sub berths and excused the driver.

"I'll walk it from here."

"Yes, sir."

His watch said 2033 hours.

Radioman, Second Class, Willie Carpenter scratched his belly and smiled up at the night sky.

Willie was three years, eleven months, and twenty days into his four-year hitch.

Ten days to go.

At six o'clock the next morning he would be aboard the air boat to Sangley Point. The following morning it was a MATS flight to Hickam, and from there T.I. and no more uniforms.

Willie had it all figured. He wasn't going back to New York and Harlem. He was staying in Frisco. With Willie's talents he could make it big in Frisco.

Hell, how many guys could shave a deck with a fingernail, deal from the middle with either hand, or double shuffle a cold deck?

In Willie's three years and eleven months, he had only taken liberty ten times, and no leave. Only fools took liberty when bored dudes were sitting around the rec area just begging for someone to take their dough.

It was a profitable four years for Willie. He had twenty-seven thousand bucks in a San Francisco bank.

No, Willie wasn't going back to Harlem, where everybody was as good as he was. Why bother? San Francisco dudes shot straight in a card game.

They were marks for Willie Carpenter.

"That you, Willie?"

"Yeah. Clover?"

"Yeah, man. What you doin' out here naked?"

"I ain't naked, man. I got my skivvies on."

"You asshole, get below. I got the aft watch. You're gonna get us both a mast!"

"Oh, shit . . ."

"Go on, Willie. You want me to put you on report?"

Jive-ass turkey, Willie thought, scrambling to his feet and moving forward.

Clover, the aft watch, moved back to the fantail.

Willie never saw the black-suited figure come up over the side and bash in the side of Clover's head.

He did see the two Marine MPs on the dock get it, and the gangway duty watch go down shortly after them.

"Jesus Christ!" he gasped, his eyes bugging as the bow and the *Shark*'s midships filled with dark figures.

He ducked down the first available hatch.

It was officers' country, but Willie disregarded the sign. He streaked down the passageway as fast as his bare feet would carry him and burst through the hatch into the officers' wardroom.

"What the hell. . . ?"

Captain McCoy and the other duty officers sat in their chairs, their heads lolling on their chests or resting on the table.

"Sheeeeit, the Russians are comin' and all the brass is takin' naps!"

Willie heard a noise in the wardroom galley and charged across the room. Through the hatch he came up short, trying to remember the seaman's name who stood in the galley screwing a silencer onto the barrel of a .45.

Then he had it.

"Clary, you got another one of those? Man, we are bein' invaded!"

Seaman, First Class, Lawrence Clary didn't reply.

He just tracked the black snout of the silencer up and pumped two hollow-points through Willie Carpenter's heart.

Pearson climbed the outer ladder and dropped to the steel deck of the tower beside Lieutenant Jacobs.

"How're we doing?"

"All secure, sir," Jacobs replied. "Only one casualty, a radioman named Carpenter. The crew is secured in the aft rec area, and Captain McCoy and the other officers have been carried down to join them."

"Excellent."

"Our men are already manning control and radar. Power is up, on-board generators are on, all running lights killed. Lifelines have been cast off except the main communications line to Harbor."

Pearson nodded and turned to the command console's glowing lights. He found the right toggle and flipped it.

"Harbor Command, this is *Shark*."

"Go ahead, *Shark*."

"All secure."

"You are clear, *Shark*."

Pearson deftly turned more dials.

"All hands, this is the captain speaking. Prepare to get underway. Chief Redding?"

"Aye, sir, we have power at full."

"Cast off bow and aft lines . . . cast off bumper lines . . . all ahead one half."

The long, sleek-bodied sub glided like a silent steel needle toward the center of the bay.

"Mr. Jacobs."

"Aye, sir?"

"When we hit the mouth of the bay, take her down to three hundred feet. From there, you know the course."

"Aye, sir."

"I'll be in my cabin. Send a sparks to me. I'll have to inform Number One that phase one of Sharkbite is completed."

FOUR

Nick Carter rolled the lightless car to a halt and sat. He was three blocks away from where Number 19 Starkley Lane should be.

He'd made London twenty minutes earlier and immediately called the MI5 number.

Sydney Jarrell patched him through, with a few curt words, to Commander Owen Hamilton.

"Bad show this, Carter. Lords was a top man."

Carter bridled, his hackles rising slightly at Hamilton's words.

The implication was clear. Carter was the outside man; it had been his job to make sure that Harry Lords, in his undercover role, didn't get wasted.

"Harry knew the game, Commander, just like I do. We all take the same chance. What have you got?"

"There are fourteen American naval officers and nine English officers currently in the U.K. with the rank of Rear Admiral and above."

"That's quite a few."

"It would be . . . now," came the reply. "There is a top meeting of air, sea, and land officers in Brussels next week. They will be planning the next year's NATO war games maneuvers and attending a top-level seminar on European defense."

"And the American military VIPs have stopped in London to plan give-and-take strategy?"

"That's correct. I have a list—"

"Save it. I'll get it later. What about Sharkbite 140-40?"

"We're working on it, and we have coordinated with Washington. Nothing yet."

"Did the housekeepers do a job on Grayburn House?"

Carter's voice was edgy, curt, and he knew it. But he didn't have time for diplomacy. Hamilton's voice, when he replied, was equally edgy but also filled with respect.

"They are going through the house now, room by room. I should have a report by noon. Some of the . . . er, casualties have been identified. We're working on the others."

There was a long pause and a slight choke in Hamilton's voice when he continued.

"My God, man, what did you use down there?"

"An M-34 grenade and a Beretta 38/49 sub, among other things."

"I thought as much. Some of them can only be identified by fingerprints, and that might prove difficult."

"Do what you can," Carter replied dryly. "What about Bridgit?"

The silence was long on the other end of the line. Carter could hear papers rattling for what seemed like forever.

"Commander . . .?"

"Yes, yes, of course. There are three Bridgits attached to MI5 Internal Security. One is an old maid of fifty-eight. She has been in records forever and is in the clear. No knowledge of the JOUST probe. Another is on public switchboard, also no knowledge."

"And the third?"

"The third is Bridgit Michaels."

"And . . . ?"

"Ms. Michaels is in Communications Liaison with MI6 and your people. It's unlikely, but she could have access to the JOUST probe through our Washington communiqués."

"Even coded?"

"That's the sticky wicket. She would also have to have access to the central codes."

"Would she?" Carter asked, his mouth suddenly very dry.

"Not likely," came the commander's nervous reply.

"She wouldn't have the clearance. But then, it has happened before. I'm ready to send a team to bring her in for interrogation."

"Don't bother," Carter said.

"Yes, I thought as much. You being an American and somewhat . . . more ruthless, I assumed you would want to see her first."

"Where?" Carter said, the image of Harry Lords's corpse clear before his eyes.

"Paddington . . . Number 19 Starkley Lane. I can give you a driver."

"Never mind, I can find it."

Carter topped off Wilhelmina's magazine and jammed it back into the Luger's butt. He slid the car keys into his pocket and stepped out into the rain-slick street.

It was almost dawn, that eerie gray light that always preceded what sunshine London got this time of year.

Two cars and a small van passed him as he moved the three blocks to Number 19, but none of the drivers seemed interested.

The only pedestrian he passed was an old lady walking a small dog. The dog yipped once and peed. The woman barely looked his way through sleepy eyes.

Number 19 was in the middle of the block. It was one of ten other five-stories, all alike.

The door at the top of a five-step stoop opened into an entryway, with a second door beyond.

The second door was locked with an old one-tumbler Yale.

Carter checked the mailboxes, found Bridgit Michaels under 3C, and picked the lock.

He walked quietly up to the third-floor landing. There was light seeping from beneath the door of 3C.

Carter went on up to the fifth floor and searched until he found the pull-down ladder that led to a trapdoor onto the roof.

Pigeons, undisturbed by the human prowler, cooed at him as he moved across tar paper and eyeballed the street below.

A Jag sedan was parked in an alleyway a block beyond

Number 19. Even if Carter had walked farther, past it, he wouldn't have made the pair hunkered down in the Jag's front and rear seats.

A little farther beyond them was the backup: an old van. Through the windshield Carter could see the glow of a cigarette.

On to Bridgit.

He took a full five minutes to case the rear of Number 19 from the roof. It backed onto an alley with similar five-story apartment houses all in a row across the way.

Nothing. At least nothing that he could see.

He chanced it and silently made his way down the fire escape.

Apartment 3C would be in the rear.

A hall door, locked from the inside, led to the fire escape itself. Off the main up-down ladder were walkways beneath the windows of the rear apartments.

Light filtered through curtains of the apartment to his right. Carter dropped to his belly and crawled along the walkway. The window ledge was even with the iron grillwork, so he only had to lift his head to peer inside.

It was a cozy living room with fairly modern furniture, not cheap. A large television dominated one corner, and one whole wall sprouted stereo equipment. A large sofa filled the opposite wall, a glass-topped coffee table in front of it.

On the coffee table was an oversize ashtray, overflowing with stubbed-out unfiltered cigarette butts.

Bridgit Michaels had spent a sleepless night.

Carter was about to move on to the next window, when the lady in question swept into the room.

She wore a feather-trimmed shorty robe that hit her just under a well-rounded rear end and flopped open in the front as she moved. Under the robe was nothing but Bridgit Michaels, and that was eye-popping enough to make Carter do a double—and then a triple—take.

Bridgit Michaels was no worn-out widow or fortyish spinster from years of indoor labor at MI5.

She was about twenty-five, with long silver-blond hair, hard blue eyes, and a perfectly shaped and robust young body.

Her agitation was obvious in the way she sucked on a freshly lit cigarette, only to crush it out and quickly light another.

When she snatched a glass from the coffee table and moved to the bar, Carter slithered to the second window.

It opened easily and silently under his touch.

The bedroom was girlishly feminine, with little stuffed dogs and Teddy bears on a large four-poster that hadn't been slept in. An open, walk-in closet revealed two long rows of London's latest in trendy chic.

Carter glimpsed four or five labels on the way by.

Bridgit Michaels had expensive taste in clothes.

At the bedroom door he paused. She was still at the bar, her back to him, shoulders hunched. The decanter of whiskey clattered against the glass as she poured.

"Make it two. It's been a long night."

The decanter crashed to the floor. It didn't break, but the amber liquid it contained spilled from its neck, creating an ugly stain on the Moroccan rug.

Bridgit Michaels whirled, her back to the bar, her ample bosom heaving on either side of the robe's fluffy trim.

There had been little sound, no more than a squeak, as her saucer-wide eyes took in Carter and her face drained of color.

Wordlessly, Carter rescued the whiskey decanter from the floor and poured three fingers into two glasses.

"Neat?" he asked, handing her one.

She nodded dumbly, taking the glass in two hands.

"Won't you sit down?" Carter asked himself, settling into the sofa. "Yes, thank you, I believe I will. How about you, Ms. Michaels?"

She walked like a robot and sat down in an opposite chair just as stiffly.

"Who . . . ?"

"Am I?" Carter finished, sipping from his glass and studying her over its rim. "Oh, I think you already know that."

"No, I—"

"Haven't your playmates outside already buzzed up to let you know that I'd arrived?"

If possible, her face went whiter. The hands holding the glass started to shake uncontrollably.

Carter leaned forward and deftly plucked the glass away. When it was safely on the coffee table, he took both her wrists in his left hand.

"Want to tell me all about it?"

"I don't know . . ."

"This is Paddington, honey . . . a working man's neighborhood. This rug we're sitting on set you back at least three thousand pounds. I'd say there's another five thousand in rags in your closet. Now you've either got a secret admirer or you're a very top-dollar hooker. Which is it?"

She tried for indignation but couldn't make it. Instead she started sputtering and attempted to free her wrists from the vise of Carter's grasp.

He squeezed hard, and then harder.

"Jesus," she cried in pain, "you're breakin' my bloody wrists!"

Carter smiled. "That's a little better. Get mad!"

"I should call the coppers . . ."

"I already have," Carter growled, squeezing her wrists until her face contorted with pain. "My name is Carter, Nick Carter. Ring a bell?"

"Let me go . . ."

She came up and Carter went with her. When she moved in close for a try for his groin, he blocked it with his hip and threw the whiskey in his right hand into her face.

She cried out and fell back into the chair of her own volition. Carter moved in over her, his face inches from hers, as she blinked and ground the burning liquid from her eyes with her knuckles.

"Harry Lords is dead, gut-shot. You know what that means, Bridgit?"

"Oh, my God . . ."

The shock in her voice and the fear that flooded her face were real.

Carter kept going.

"A slug in the gut is the most painful, agonizing way to die. It takes a long time to go that way, Bridgit. It digs and burns, and if it doesn't go all the way through to rupture your spine, you can live a whole hour or more before you bleed to death on the inside."

He unholstered Wilhelmina, levered a shell into the chamber, and dropped the Luger's muzzle between the lines of feather trim. He found the valley between her full breasts and moved the cold steel down until he found her navel.

"Oh, dear Jesus, you wouldn't . . ." she choked, sweat popping from every pore of her body.

"Wouldn't I? Harry Lords wasn't the only one who bought it tonight, lady. An even dozen of JOUST's best went with him. Guess who delivered 'em."

"You . . . you killed twelve men?"

"In about twenty-four minutes. That's two minutes a kill, Bridgit . . . about the same time it's going to take for you if you don't start talking."

Bridgit started talking. It was the usual story but slightly more odd in Bridgit's case, because it's usually men, not women, who get addicted to gambling and the fast life.

Beautiful, not very smart, and out for kicks.

"What's the name of the club?"

"The Mainstem. It's on Charing Cross Road, near Soho."

"I've heard of it."

"I was several thousand pounds in debt when a man came here to see me. He was very understanding and told me that in exchange for certain information he could arrange to have not only my debts wiped out, but he'd fix it so I'd get a sizable monthly retainer."

Carter looked around the apartment. "Very sizable, I'd say."

She nodded and color—lots of red—returned to her face.

"Someone high up arranged for a different position for me at MI5. I was given keys to the code room, and now and then an assignment that would keep me in the building beyond my watch."

Little bells went off in Carter's brain. Obviously, if an MI5 employee could be manipulated from inside, there was someone else—besides Bridgit—on the inside.

"Who was the guy who contacted you?"

"He said his name was Styles. That's all, just Styles."

"English or American?"

"That was the odd of it. He was American. Also . . ."

"Yes?"

"I think he had something to do with the American Navy. He was always dropping navy terms. I recognized them because my brother was a seaman. May I . . . uh . . ."

"What?"

"Have another drink?"

"Help yourself."

Carter removed Wilhelmina's muzzle from her belly and settled himself back into the sofa to think.

It was difficult.

As she moved to the bar, the white-feathered hem of her short robe shimmied with each bounce of her round buttocks.

Carter studied her as he lit a cigarette.

She was beautiful, almost too beautiful, in a hard way. As a playgirl moving in the same circles of the London jet set, she could have easily become a well-kept plaything.

It would have been a lot easier than the game she was playing now.

Bridgit returned to the chair across from Carter, sat, and crossed her legs.

She had regained some of her calm, not to mention decorum.

When she caught the look in Carter's eyes as they traveled up her bare thighs, she quickly uncrossed them and tugged uselessly at the robe's short hem.

"I think you've been telling me part of the truth. What's the rest of it?"

She chewed a little on a very ample lower lip and kept her eyes on the amber liquid in her glass.

"I did get a phone call last night, but not from any men outside."

"From whom then?"

"Styles. He told me that some plans had gone awry. He didn't know how much you had learned, if anything."

"That would have been the mess at Grayburn House. Go on."

"He said if you did happen to show up, I was to . . ."

"Well?"

"Seduce you, if possible, and put these in your drink."

She opened her hand to reveal two cellophane-wrapped tablets in her palm.

"Why didn't you? Seduce me, I mean."

"I was going to. But the way you came in . . . the gun. I was shocked and scared. I still am."

"I suppose you're telling me you don't know what JOUST was all about?"

"I don't, I swear! This JOUST was only one of the items I was supposed to monitor."

"What were the others?"

"Mercenary recruitment in the U.K., dossiers on military personnel suspected of heavy right-wing leanings. And . . . oh, yes, anything to do with Lady Grayburn."

"That would all fit in. And I'll bet there was one other thing . . ."

"Yes," she nodded, working even harder on the lip. "Any efforts to subvert or infiltrate JOUST."

And then the tears came.

"But I swear I didn't know that it would all lead to such

killing! Styles even told me that, in a way, I would be serving my country."

"I'm sure some of them really think that way," Carter said dryly. "What about 'Sharkbite'?"

"What?"

"Okay, what about the three, maybe more, on your doorstep?"

"I didn't know they were out there until you told me. Of course, I guess I could have supposed when Styles called . . ."

Carter leaned forward and lifted the packets from her hand. "What was the deal if you got these down me?"

"They gave me a number to call."

"And if you didn't?"

"The other way"—she swallowed—"was the seduction. When it was over . . . in bed, I mean . . . I was to excuse myself to go to the loo. It's at the front end of the hall."

"And?"

"If I had gotten you to bed, I was to wave a towel out the front hall window."

"Then what?"

She shrugged. "Leave my front door unlocked, return to bed, and keep you there until someone came to arrest you for interrogation."

"Damn, what guts they've got!" Carter hissed. "Arrest me?"

"And if I wasn't able to do either one—give you the pills or seduce you—I was to deny everything and then scream like hell until you left or my neighbors intervened."

Carter leaned back on the sofa, squinting his eyes, his mind clicking off all Bridgit had said and all it meant.

He had a pretty good hunch the pills in his hand were a lot more than knockout drops. Once in his belly he would probably have lived only another minute.

If it had come down to the third alternative, her screaming, they would probably have nailed him coming out of the building.

What would they have done, or do, if she had been on his arm?

That left the seduction.

"Bridgit . . ."

"Yes?"

"You're in deep. And if you've been telling me the truth, I don't think you know just how deep. This outfit plays for high stakes, and for keeps."

"I didn't know Harry Lords, and I swear I didn't know he would be killed."

"But you did know you were violating the Official Secrets Act."

Again the high-cheekboned, model-beautiful face drained of color. "Yes. But they kept assuring me that really I was doing nothing wrong. In the end, they said, I would be doing my country a great service."

Carter felt a little ill. If what she said were true, then why accept so much money for her treachery? Why not do it just for Queen and Country? That's what he wanted to say.

But he didn't.

There was a better way to dish up reality.

"Have you got a wig?"

"What?"

"A wig . . . have you got one?"

"Yes. Sometimes I don't have time to do my hair, so—"

"Get it," Carter rasped, cutting her off. "And get your towel ready."

FIVE

Carter crouched in the closet, the scent from Bridgit Michaels's clothing filling his nostrils. The sap he had almost used on the shooter at Grayburn House was in his right hand.

Just in case, Wilhelmina occupied his left.

No lights were on in the living room or the bedroom. A narrow shaft of sunlight seeped through a crack in the drapes to fall across the hanks of hair on the pillow and the sheet covering the wadded blankets serving as bodies.

The door from the living room to the bedroom was open about six inches and within Carter's sight.

It had been about ten minutes since Bridgit had done her towel-waving routine from the front window. Now she was dressed and crouching on the fire escape outside the window.

"What if the neighbors across the way see me?" she had asked.

"Wave to them. You're just getting some early morning air."

For ten seconds and ten seconds only, Carter had thought about calling Hamilton and MI5 for backup. But if there was another leak in MI5 besides Bridgit, it would do little good . . . and maybe blow the whole thing.

A creak of wood . . . faint, barely discernible . . . but there.

It was the front door of the apartment.

Carter tensed, relaxed, and tensed his muscles again to get them ready.

The bedroom door moved an inch, and then another six inches.

The first thing through the opening was the silenced snout of a Heckler and Koch UP70 machine pistol. Like everything else the West Germans manufactured, the UP70 was a work of art.

It operated on selective three-round bursts from an eighteen-round feeder at a deadly cyclic rate of 2,200 rounds per minute.

Just as fast as the trigger could be pulled.

The man behind the UP70 was young, wearing jeans and a baggy pullover. The sweater had probably been used to hide the machine pistol across the street and up the stairs to 3C.

His all-night vigil showed. His lean, deeply tanned face badly needed a shave.

He moved toward the bed with startling economy. So much so that it seemed as if no part of him moved except the extended arm holding the pistol.

When the hand holding the UP70 was just over the foot of the bed, the long silencer began bucking. The room was filled with the smell of burned powder and the dull thud of the slugs as they tore into the heavy blankets.

Nick Carter was a pro. He recognized another one.

The guy took no chances. He just kept firing.

Carter counted the bursts in his head: . . . four . . . five . . . six.

Three times six is eighteen—exactly what the UP70 magazine held.

The shooter was just moving around the bed on Carter's side to check his handiwork when Killmaster moved out.

The guy was sharp.

Carter's gliding steps barely made a sound on the rug, but he heard them.

The sap was aimed for the soft spot behind his ear. Carter would have settled for the back of the skull, but he didn't even get that.

In turning, the shooter had ground his head reflexively down between his shoulders and raised one arm to stop the sap.

He growled like a wounded tiger when the lump of lead

caught his elbow, but he was still able to swing the machine pistol toward his attacker's head.

Carter bent backward to escape the blow and brought the sap down sharply on the other man's wrist.

Bones broke and the UP70 clattered to the floor.

But the guy still wasn't out. He wasn't even down. With his left arm hanging uselessly at his side, he dived.

The toe of Carter's boot caught him square in the kneecap, but the shooter still managed to catch Carter head on. They both tumbled to the floor.

Carter barely managed to avoid two fingers in his eye sockets by lurching his head forward and catching them on his forehead. Even then the blow sent a minor shock wave clear to the back of his head.

He was tempted to just squeeze one off from the Luger and be done with it.

But he didn't.

Carter wanted at least one prisoner if he could get one.

He gave the guy a quick one-two: Wilhelmina across the right side of his head, and then the sap across the bridge of his nose.

This time there was no scream of pain, not even a growl of defiance. Just a grunt and he was out.

Carter pushed him the rest of the way from his body with his knees and stood.

Bridgit crouched at the window, her hands holding the drapes open, her head a few inches inside.

"Did . . . you . . . kill him?"

Carter checked. The guy was an ox. He was bleeding badly and probably had at least one concussion, but his pulse was steady as a rock.

"No, I'm afraid not. Do you know him?"

She crawled the rest of the way through the window and crossed the room.

"Oh, God, he looks awful."

"That's because his nose is bashed in." Carter twisted the shooter's face around and mopped it partially clean with the edge of the sheet. "There."

"Yes, I know him . . . not his name, but I know him.

He was . . . is . . . a bouncer at the Mainstem Club."

"Where you lost your dough?"

"Yes. Oh, God, did you have to do that to him? I mean, he was always so nice to me."

"Come here," Carter growled, dropping the gunman's head and grabbing Bridgit's wrist. He yanked her to the side of the bed and pushed her face down toward the blankets. "What the hell do you think those are?"

She looked at the holes in the bedding, and then realization flooded her face.

"Bullet holes."

"Yeah. Big ones. And you'll notice they stitch across the bed from side to side."

Carter didn't have to elaborate that if they had both been in that bed they would have been very dead now.

Bridgit rolled out of his grasp and sat on the bed hugging herself with her arms. She looked as if she was going to be sick.

Carter didn't wait.

He went through the unconscious man's pockets, transferring everything he found into his own except an extra clip for the UP70.

Then he darted into the living room and ripped the draws from Bridgit's expensive drapes.

When the would-be killer was securely trussed up on the floor, he searched and found the machine pistol. Once the new magazine was locked in, he moved back to Bridgit.

"Hey . . ."

She sat zombielike, staring from the shooter's mashed face to the holes in the sheet. Her body was quaking like a leaf in a heavy breeze.

"Hey . . . you!" Carter yelled, shaking her until her teeth were rattling in her pretty jaw.

"Y-yes . . . I'm sorry."

"Okay, take this." He shoved the machine pistol into her hands. "It's a gun. It goes bang-bang and kills people."

"What . . . ?"

"He's tied, but he's a hotshot, probably full of tricks. If he moves or tries to get up, just point this at him and squeeze. It'll do the rest. And don't try it out unless you have to. These damn things don't have a safety."

"What are you going to do?"

"Take care of his backup."

Carter headed for the window. Her voice stopped him halfway.

"They'll put me in prison, won't they?"

"What?"

"For violating the Official Secrets Act."

She looked pitiful, pathetic. Mascara was all over her face, and her eyes were red-rimmed and swollen. The white sweater and slacks she wore were all smudged from the fire escape outside.

Suddenly she wasn't beautiful anymore.

She was just hard . . . and used.

Yeah, Carter thought, *she should have been a hooker. It's what she was really cut out for.*

"Won't they?"

"Maybe not," he replied. "I'll put in a good word."

And then he was gone, out the window and up the fire escape to the roof.

There had been something in her eyes, in the sardonic twist of her lips when Carter looked at her one last time before going through the window.

He should have known, guessed.

But other things were pounding in his head.

The shooter in 3C and all of his buddies in the street had had a good look at Carter's face.

If possible, he didn't want them carrying a description back to Number One.

From the roof, Carter did a recon of the street.

It was Sunday morning, and bells were ringing all over Paddington.

But Starkley Lane and its adjacent, narrow side streets were almost deserted.

The van was still parked in the same place. Carter could

see an image behind its semidarkened glass, but only one.

The Jaguar was still in the alley, but it was empty.

Carter knew that one of its former occupants was in 3C.

But where was the other one?

He moved low, over the roofs to the end of the block.

From there he spotted him: a tall, rangy guy, also in jeans and a blousey sweater. He leaned casually against the stoop of Number 19, smoking a cigarette and occasionally glancing over his shoulder into the hallway.

Neither of the watchers could see the Jag where it was parked in the alley.

Carter formulated a quick plan and moved.

He used the fire escape of the end building and hit the alley running. Three blocks down he turned and came out on Starkley Lane. He was fifty yards beyond his car.

"Fish an' chips, sar?"

He was shorter than Carter and a little wider, with a fringe of gray beneath the brimmed straw on his head. The white coat he wore was long, nearly to his knees, and the two-wheeled cart he pushed with charcoal smoke pouring from under its glass top was heaven sent.

"Don't want no chips, mate," Carter said in a blend of Cockney-Soho. "But ah'd like ta rent yer coat, hat, and cart fer a bit."

"What fer, lad?"

"Me old woman an' me's divorcin', we are."

"So?"

"So she's locked me outta the house, she has. An' she's put me kip in the boot o' that Ford there. Fellow up there on the stoop's a hard one, he is . . . boxer, her boyfriend."

"Oh, ah've got ya, lad," the old man said with a knowing chuckle.

"All I want's me kip."

"Ten quid, lad, but don't ya get me business busted up!"

"I'll handle 'er like a babe, ah will."

They traded coats, and Carter jammed the skimmer

down hard on his head, then sauntered off with the pushcart.

At the rear of the Ford, he lifted the glass top of the cart and made motions of cooking. Steam and smoke billowed into the air, but the watcher on the stoop hardly gave him a glance.

Twice he leaned down by the side of the cart and came up with more fish fillets. The third time he opened the Ford's trunk and grabbed the pouch containing the sulfurous flashes and the grenades. With the pouch under the coat and tucked into his belt, Carter moved back up and across the street.

"Chips . . . fish an' chips!" he called.

He turned the corner and looked across at the old man, who had stayed out of sight behind the end building. Carter waved him over and chuckled to himself at the ham in the old codger as he whistled his way across the street with his hands in his pockets.

"Slick ye are, lad. Ya should be a dipper!"

"Who knows, mate," Carter laughed, shoving two ten-pound notes into the old man's hand, "ah might be!"

He ran down the block, took a left and counted off three blocks at a steady jog. In the middle of the fourth block he slowed and then stopped to peer around the corner down the alley.

The Jag was still there.

In no time he had the passenger door open and was lying across the front floorboard.

With his head and part of his shoulders up under the dash, Carter wedged one of the grenades up into the maze of wires. When he was sure it was secure and wouldn't dislodge easily, he traced the antenna wire from the radio to its outside connector.

With both ends unscrewed, he used Hugo to cut off the connectors and then clean the insulation from the stiff inner wire core.

One end he attached to the pin of the grenade. The other he rolled and mashed until it was wadded into a ball. He then stuffed it into the rubber lip under the accelerator.

Carefully he pressed the pedal to make sure that the tension, when the time came, would be enough to pull the M-34 pin.

Finished, he slid from the Jaguar and retraced his route back to where he had paid off and left the old man with the fish and chips cart.

What he was about to do was risky, but only to Carter and the men from JOUST.

The hour was still early enough that the streets in this area of Paddington were empty. No civilians would be threatened.

He set himself at the corner, gripped the ignition keys in his hand, and sprinted.

Carter was in the Ford and moving before the guy on the stoop caught on. The man sprinted in front of the car and ran for the Jag as fast as his legs would carry him.

Carter slowed as he neared the van, glancing at it just long enough to make sure it held only one occupant.

It did, and he was wrestling the wheel like hell to make a U-turn.

Carter stayed in second, making a lot of noise but not too much speed. In the rearview mirror he saw the van coming on fast and then saw the Jag whip out of the alley behind him.

An M-34 has a four-to-six-minute fuse delay. All three cars had made two turns and were about four blocks from Number 19 when the Jag blew. It lifted ten feet into the air and came down on its top in the middle of the street.

There was no flame or smoke. Just turning wheels, crushed metal, and a mangled body.

In his rearview mirror Carter could see the confusion on the van driver's face.

His face would register one hell of a lot more than that in the next few minutes.

Carter floored the Ford in third, made another turn, and headed for a small park. The van was right on his tail and jumped the curve right behind Carter.

Carter slewed to the right, went between two trees, and zigzagged back to his left.

The van followed him, skidding hard at the trees. One fender caught, but the driver barreled on through.

In the center of the park was a small lake. Once Carter had the little Ford righted, he made directly for the water. The grass was still dewy soft, making it hard for the cumbersome van to track directly behind Carter now.

By the time Carter was thirty yards from the pond, the van was behind him another fifty.

Just short of plunging into the drink, Carter brodied the Ford left, shifted into neutral, and stood on the brakes. He did a complete hundred-and-eighty-degree turn and came to a halt nose-to-nose with the onrushing van.

Carter tumbled from the car, groping with both hands in the pouch.

Shock and amazement filled the driver's face as he saw his prey actually running in the open toward the pond.

He geared down for more control and veered away from the Ford after the running figure.

At the water's edge, Carter stopped and spun around. He swung his right and then his left arm in two perfect, pitching arcs.

Killmaster N3 was already on one knee, Wilhelmina filling his hands, his eyes shut tightly, when the flashes went off right in front of the van's windshield and the driver's eyes.

The blinding glare lasted only a split second, but it was long enough to blind the driver. His hands left the steering wheel to dig into the pain that had flooded his eyes.

Without guidance, the soft mud beneath the front wheels at the water's edge turned them. The van slid into a broadside directly toward Carter.

Carter's eyes were open now and tracking over the Luger's sights.

The first shot was high, zinging off the edge of the roof, leaving a crease.

Carter tracked down and squeezed off two more. They

both found their marks, one directly in the driver's left ear, the other tearing off a good chunk of his skull.

Carter lunged to the side and rolled clear as the van slid by him. It hit the water, went up on two wheels, and then, in slow motion, eased over onto its side.

Carter didn't even look back as he ran to the Ford. There was no need. He had already seen clearly what the twin 9mms had done.

Slowly, keeping well within the speed laws and casually smoking a cigarette, Carter drove back to the alley behind Number 19 Starkley Lane.

In the same unhurried manner, he climbed the fire escape to the third floor and edged along the walkway to the bedroom of 3C.

"Bridgit . . . ?"

Silence.

"It's me, Bridgit . . . don't get nervous with that toy . . ."

Still no reply.

Carter checked the buildings opposite, saw no curious faces, and slipped Wilhelmina from her sheath. Slowly he edged closer to the window.

And then he saw it. Blood on the sill.

Quickly he doubled back to the living room window, slid it open, and silently moved inside, the Luger ready.

The silence seemed to thunder in his ears as he tiptoed to the bedroom door.

It was tricky; there was no way to roll through the door without being in a direct firing line from anywhere in the other room.

"Bridgit . . ." he called again, casting his eyes around the living room.

Her purse sat on top of the nearby television. Carter emptied it on the floor and snatched up the compact. Flipping it open, he left a trail of powder across the Moroccan rug as he moved back to the door.

Gingerly he moved his hand holding the compact mirror into the opening. The skin on his wrist tingled, expecting a slug to shatter the mirror, his hand, or both.

A hand was better than his head.

The area under the window was clear, as was the closet.

The bed wasn't.

Bridgit Michaels sprawled grotesquely across the bullet-holed sheet and bundled blankets.

Still curious, Carter dropped the compact and rolled into the room, scanning with the business end of the Luger.

Nobody home but Bridgit . . . or what was left of her.

Carter checked her pulse out of habit, but he knew there was no need. Raw red marks encircled her throat. He could tell without examining her further that Bridgit Michaels's neck was broken.

The bedroom shooter had a strong right arm.

Standing there, looking down at her bloodless, once pretty face, Carter could almost re-create the whole scene in his mind.

Fear, confusion, stupidity, and her own blind desire for survival at any cost had been the killer's ally.

Carter could almost hear him talking to the bewildered girl with calm certainty.

Hadn't they stood by her and protected her to this point?

They were a powerful organization. There would be no question of her going to prison if she continued to help them.

He probably even offered her the moon and Jamaica or Bermuda.

She had set the machine pistol down and moved with quaking limbs to untie her liberator.

Only at the last second he had turned from liberator to killer. His right hand had found her throat, and her neck under his powerful grip had probably snapped like a twig.

SIX

The ashtray at Carter's right hand was approaching half full, and his belly burned from too much coffee. But not any more than his eyes. They were red-rimmed and watery from lack of sleep and studying file photos of every MI5 employee from file clerks to field agents.

The round, white-faced, sterile clock on the wall read 3:00. He had been at it for nearly three hours.

He had left the mess at 19 Starkley Lane and driven directly to the MI5 headquarters at Leconfield House near Park Lane.

Once through security checks, he had been ushered abruptly into the Spartan office of Commander Owen Hamilton. It was the first time in the long probe of JOUST that Carter had met Hamilton face-to-face. Both Lords and Carter had been in the cold, with all their communications done through underlings or by phone.

The commander, Carter decided at first sight, fitted the setting of his office and his reputation.

He was extremely tall and bone thin, with stone gray hair and skin the texture of parchment drawn over gaunt facial bones. He might have been in his late fifties or early sixties. It was impossible to gauge.

Hamilton greeted Carter with formal British courtesy that quickly went by the wayside when Carter related his latest meeting with JOUST at 19 Starkley Lane.

"Good God, man, you've turned a peaceful country manor outside Cardiff into a killing ground, and now you've done the same with a London street! And this last affair in broad daylight . . ."

The commander was just getting warmed up. He castigated Carter for the next fifteen minutes, telling him that London was not the Wild West and that there had been enough of this brand of violence by the IRA. The people of London, as well as the government, would not stand for much more of it.

Carter stood, listening to every word and, now and then, solemnly nodding his agreement. When he was pretty sure Hamilton had run out of gas, he replied verbally.

"You're quite right, sir—"

"Damn right, I'm right."

"My apologies to the people of London, you, your staff, and the Queen. May I sit down now, sir? My legs are a little beat."

"Of course. Care for a brandy?"

"That would taste good."

For the next hour, Commander Hamilton briefed Carter on what they had gleaned from Grayburn House.

Most of the JOUST "soldiers" were highly trained ex-military men from the U.K., France, and the United States. To a man, they had all been connected at one time or another with mercenary groups around the world after their regular tours of duty were finished.

Complete background checks hadn't been completed on all of them as yet. But from what had been done, a pattern was emerging.

None of them had ever made a secret of his almost fanatical anti-Communist thinking or of his activities. Several of them had enlisted in Africa under General Helmut Gregor to fight Communist-backed guerrillas.

Carter had heard a lot about Helmut Gregor. The man was far less than subtle.

He had been ushered out of the United States Army after a tour of duty in Vietnam.

The reason: cruelty that bordered on sadism.

In the regular army he had never gone beyond the rank of captain. In his own mercenary army, he had declared himself a general.

Before he was finally killed—many suspected that he was assassinated—Gregor had become an embarrassment to the U.S. government as well as to several other Western governments who were trying to reach peaceful solutions through diplomacy in several emerging African Third World countries.

War—and total annihilation of the enemy—was for Gregor the only solution. If there was no war, he would create one so the enemy could be killed.

Without stating the fact, both Carter and Commander Owen Hamilton knew that if a high percentage of JOUST's "elite corps" had followed General Gregor, their new leader was probably every bit as radical.

Grayburn House had been stripped bare. Nothing had been found that would pinpoint the identity of the mysterious admiral or, as he had been called by one of his men, Number One.

Scotland Yard, Customs, and Special Branch had been alerted to Lady Lenore Grayburn's part in the affair. Orders had been issued to arrest and detain the lady on sight.

But now, with the realization of just how tangled and how far-reaching JOUST was, it was assumed that she would be far underground and impossible to find.

Commander Hamilton passed Carter the list of military names he had accumulated earlier that morning.

Carter scanned down the names and the thumbnail sketches of each man. Immediately he excised ten of the names. The ten were rear admirals. He was positive the rank he had observed on Number One's sleeve was higher than the lowest admiralty rank.

"May I keep this list? I'd like to study it further."

"Of course."

Carter lit another cigarette and pondered the next move. "Nothing from Washington on Sharkbite 140-40?"

"Not yet," Hamilton replied, "but it has top priority with both your people and ours."

Carter nodded. "It's a waiting game then. I might as well spend it usefully."

"How so?"

"By going through your MI5 personnel files. Maybe something will jar loose, and we can find out who Bridgit Michaels's unknown control was in your organization."

Hamilton's face reddened somewhat, but he nodded his agreement. "We also have people watching this Mainstem Club, for all the good it will do."

"I imagine if there were any JOUST connections there, they've gone under by now. But I would like to check it out myself later tonight when the action starts."

"I'll set up a backup for you with Special Branch."

Then Carter was led into a small office and furnished with six heavy tomes of MI5 personnel.

He was now on book five, and the photographs were all running together.

The person behind the voice of Sydney Jarrell sat across from him.

"I think you've about had it, old chap. Your eyes are drooping."

"I know, but there are only two to go," Carter replied, turning pages and concentrating.

In the few hours they had just spent together, the former friction between the men had turned to respect.

"Wait a minute . . ."

"Got something?"

"I'm not sure. Can you put this one up on the screen and blow it up?"

"Right-o," Jarrell replied, already reaching for an interoffice phone.

"And also . . . get an artist in here."

A half hour later, Carter was sure of it.

They had projected the man's picture on a three-by-five screen. An artist had removed the mustache and had sketched in heavy, horn-rimmed glasses.

There was no doubt of it. The man in the picture was the same man who had escaped Carter at Grayburn House in the little Jaguar. His name was Harley Donne.

"It would fit," Jarrell mused. "He's in Personnel Evaluation, and his military service was in Communication Intelligence. He's an amateur operator now. Here's his dossier."

Carter scanned it.

Good school, strong background. No sports, but a very high academic achiever. Six years military service. Not outstanding, but flawless in conduct and job rating.

Jarrell was just replacing the phone when Carter looked up.

"He's on holiday . . . has been for the past two weeks."

Carter smiled. "I guess he'll be on permanent holiday now, don't you?"

"I do," Jarrell nodded, "but I'll have his flat checked out just in case."

"And dig into his personal habits for the last couple of years—friends, relatives, where he spent his last holidays—anything you can get."

"Will do."

Commander Hamilton and an aide came brusquely through the door.

"Scrambler line from Washington, Nick. Priority One. It's your chief. You can take it in my office."

"Chief" meant David Hawk, head of ultrasecret AXE, and the call would be coming from Dupont Circle.

"Carter here."

"Ginger, Nick . . . one sec."

Ginger was Hawk's right hand, Ginger Bateman: beautiful, intelligent, and a woman of few words.

"N3?"

"Here."

"We've got us one hell of a can of worms."

A man of Nicholas Carter's expertise and background is rarely awed. By the end of David Hawk's two-minute recitation of that day's events at Subic Bay, Carter was properly awed.

"Holy . . . they hijacked a nuclear sub?"

"Along with four missiles with nuclear warheads and the devices to arm them."

"Is it a ransom deal?"

"If JOUST is in it," Hawk growled, "it's ten-to-one they've got more in mind than ransom."

Hawk sounded more than just tense, and Carter could understand why.

"We're monitoring all frequencies now, just in case they break radio silence. Last sight of them was off the northern coast of Luzon, in the Philippines. They surfaced just long enough to put the crew ashore in rubber boats."

"Any ideas on their direction?" Carter asked, choked tenseness creeping into his own voice.

"None. We put Pac Fleet Command on it, and ships in that area are trying to get a fix. An AWAC is also making time toward that area of the Pacific, but that will take time."

"Do we have anything?"

"The crew identified four of their own as the on-board mutineers: two officers and two enlisted men. Their names and service records are on their way to you now. In the meantime, we're digging here. Have you got anything?"

"Damn little beyond what we've already sent," Carter replied.

"Stay on it from that end, Nick, and keep us informed hourly here. It's pins and needles time until we find out what the hell they want with an armed nuclear submarine. But I have a hunch we'll find out all too soon. One second . . ."

Hawk left the line for a full minute. When he came back on, there was even more gravity in his voice.

"The President has informed Moscow."

"And . . . ?"

"We have full cooperation from the Kremlin. They are joining in the search."

Little wheels clicked in Carter's brain.

"Could JOUST be planning . . . ?"

"World War Three?" Hawk growled. "It's a frightening supposition, but one we have to live with. Get on the admirals, Nick. If we can find out who the hell this

Number One is, maybe we can talk some sense into the idiot before there's a big bang."

Carter's hands, as he replaced the receiver, were sweating.

SEVEN

The Mainstem was not the plushest of London's many gambling clubs, but it was one of the most exclusive.

Special Branch provided Carter with a government steward's card, which was honored without question at the door. Announcing himself as an inspector of the London Gambling Commission would make his every move while in the club monitored, but, in many ways, that was better.

They would be watching Carter watch the games, and not be cognizant of the fact that he was spending his time watching the players and employees.

A fast check of the Mainstem's license hadn't revealed much. Like their Las Vegas counterparts, the ownership of a gambling club is partially submerged in murky corporate alleyways.

The nominal owner and front for the corporate ownership was Anthony Adamo. He was an American from New York but was now a naturalized British citizen.

A glass-paneled door led to the inner sanctum of the club. It was a small, tastefully furnished gaming room, with an oak-paneled bar along one wall and the tables themselves in the center.

As in all European casinos, the sound was muted. There was no rattle of one-armed bandits or loud voices, only the click of chips and a low hum of conversation.

All the croupiers, bartenders, and waiters were dressed in tuxedoes, as were the male customers, including Carter. Costly designer gowns and real jewelry attested to the status of the women players.

Only one small, red-haired waiter took any notice of Carter as he moved across the room to the bar.

The barstools were all empty. Carter chose an end one. He had barely covered the stool when the bartender—a bored-looking man with thick eyebrows that needed combing—set a cocktail napkin before him.

"Your order, sir?"

"Whiskey . . . neat."

The drink arrived. Carter sipped and swiveled around on the stool to survey the room.

He had made one sweep with his eyes when a tall blonde in a powder blue evening gown slid onto a stool three down from his.

Carter glanced once and then looked . . . hard.

She was a woman in every meaning of the word. Her hair was a natural ash blond, and her face boasted a haughty patrician profile. Her face and shoulders were deeply tanned, showing off the color of her hair to perfection.

She was by far the most beautiful woman in the room.

And then Carter realized she was also the drunkest.

The bored bartender was giving her a hard time.

"I said I wanted a goddamned drink!"

"But I've already told you, Mrs.—"

"I *know* you've told me, and now that you have, you've fulfilled your little lackey duties. So move your ass and pour me a scotch . . . a double!"

The bartender shook his head and moved away. He went through the motions of making her drink, but Carter saw him talking rapidly with his head and eyes to the club's beefy bouncer.

The woman was dumping the contents of her beaded handbag on the bar in a vain effort to find fire for the cigarette that drooped from the corner of her mouth. In so doing, her misty gaze floated over to Carter.

"What the hell are you looking at?"

"You."

"What's the matter, haven't you ever seen a drunk before?"

"None quite as beautiful as you."

"*Touché* . . . gotta light?"

Carter fished his lighter out. But instead of moving to her and lighting the cigarette, he slid the lighter down the bar. "Help yourself."

"Thanks," she said, with an eyebrow-lifting smile.

With smoke rolling from her narrow nostrils, she returned the lighter and dismissed Carter by turning away. The bartender delivered her drink and then answered the back bar phone.

Carter strained but could not hear the conversation. Hanging up the phone, the bartender motioned a waiter over. The waiter nodded, and Carter carefully followed his progress from the bar.

"Mr. Styles . . . telephone for Mr. Styles . . ."

He repeated it at every gaming table and then at every drinking table along the far side of the room.

Not one man looked up or even glanced at the waiter as he passed.

Well, Carter thought, *so much for Mr. Styles tipping his hand*. Whoever had recruited Bridgit Michaels was either not in the Mainstem this evening or had already skipped the country.

"Buzz off, fatso. I want another drink."

The blonde was again irate. This time her anger was directed at a dark, squat man with black, piercing eyes and salt and pepper gray hair. The tuxedo he wore was carefully tailored, but it couldn't hide the enormous paunch that protruded from the jacket.

Behind him, hovering over his shoulder like a mountain of flesh and bone, was the doorman-bouncer.

The main man was grinning, but it wasn't a grin of humor. His cheeks hung like squirrel pouches, and the feeble attempt at a smile only made them hang lower.

"My dear Mrs. Pearson, I am indeed sorry, but I'm afraid you'll have to leave."

"You heard me, Tony, I said buzz off! And take your muscle with you!"

Carter figured the paunchy man for Anthony Adamo.

But what sent a tingle of alarm and interest up Carter's spine was the woman's name: Pearson.

Mrs. Pearson.

He wondered if this attractive, obviously very American blonde could be any relation to Lieutenant Commander Ralph Pearson, who was at this very moment playing skipper of the shanghaied U.S.S. *Shark* somewhere under the Pacific Ocean.

Before leaving the MI5 headquarters earlier that afternoon for a shower and a few, much needed hours of sleep, Carter had gone over the background records and dossiers on the four U.S. Navy men who had taken part in the theft of the *Shark*.

Now he put the computer part of his brain to work.

Ralph Pearson had been a model cadet at the Academy. He had graduated in the top tenth of his class at Annapolis and then had gone on to submarine school. He had also excelled there, and after two years of sea duty he had been reassigned to M.I.T. for graduate work in physics.

His specialty had been nuclear ordnance, and by the time he was graduated and had returned to duty, he was considered an expert.

All well and good, except that Carter was now interested in a different aspect of Pearson's background: his personal life.

He blotted out everything in the room, squinting his eyes and concentrating.

And then he had it.

Her first name was Elise. Maiden name, Tyson. She was the socialite daughter of the late Milford Tyson, wealthy resident of Virginia's horse country and twice an unsuccessful candidate for the U.S. Senate.

Elise Tyson and Ralph Pearson had been married five years before, just after he had finished his graduate studies at M.I.T.

That had been the extent of the lady's personal background in her husband's file.

Carter made a mental note to do some further digging.

But right now the argument Adamo and Mrs. Pearson

were having had escalated into a shouting match. Heads were turning from the other tables, and the fat little man's face was getting extremely red.

After a particularly vehement exchange, he balled his fists at his sides and puffed himself up until, even with his fat neck, the cords of his throat stood out.

Finally he stomped away.

Elise Pearson—if this lady was indeed Elise Pearson—shot him an obscene gesture and turned back to her drink.

Carter smiled to himself. The lady was earthy, even a bit crude, but she had a mind of her own.

Carter moved in.

"Excuse me . . ." he said in a very clipped Oxbridge accent.

"Yeah?"

"At one time I traveled to the States quite often."

"Big deal. Got another light?"

Carter lit her cigarette and continued in the soft nasal accent.

"Several times, while in the States, I dropped into the Hunt Club south of Arlington . . ."

Her face came up, and for the first time her bleary eyes focused directly on Carter. "Yeah?"

"Quite. Please don't think me forward, but I do believe we've met. Elise Tyson . . . ?"

"Once. Now I'm Elise Pearson. My husband's in the Navy. He loves boats and playing war games. He even does it in the bathtub."

"Oh. Stationed here in the U.K., is he?"

"No, I don't know where the hell he's stationed."

You'll know, Carter thought, *just as soon as the press gets wind of what's going down on the other side of the world.*

"It is a small world," Carter said, putting as much lightness in his voice as he could muster. "My name is Dobbins . . . Cedric Dobbins. May I buy you a drink?"

"No thanks, I buy my own drinks. Excuse me . . . the drinks are taking their toll on my bladder."

She slid from the stool and moved toward the rear of the room and the alcove to the restrooms. Even as inebriated as she was, the movement beneath the dress was fluidly smooth and extremely feminine.

Carter watched until she disappeared, then lit a cigarette to wait. Somehow—he didn't know yet—he was going to get close to Mrs. Elise Pearson before the evening was over.

"Another drink, sir?"

"Yes, please."

Carter finished the cigarette, and then another. Nearly ten minutes had passed since Elise Pearson had answered nature's call.

Even for a woman, that was too long.

Carter slid from his own perch and moved through the now crowded tables.

Inside the first door was a short hallway, with *Mesdames* on one side and *Monsieurs* on the other. There was a door at the end of the hall marked Private.

Carter strained an ear at the *Mesdames* door for several seconds, heard nothing, and entered the door across the hall.

The place was empty.

At the lavatory he washed his hands. Just as he was drying them, the waiter with the red hair stepped through the door and came up to his side.

He rolled a wallet open in his right hand and held the index finger of his left up to his lips.

The wallet contained a shield and an ID card, complete with picture identifying him as Claude Dakin, Special Branch.

Carter nodded and shrugged, furrowing his brows toward the finger at the man's lips. The wallet disappeared, and Dakin pointed to the two top screws seemingly holding the large mirror into the wall.

Carter spotted them immediately as two small microphones.

Again he nodded his understanding and followed the agent to the five urinals that lined the walls. Carter got the picture. Working together, they flushed all five until the room was reverberating with the sound of rushing, gurgling water.

Dakin was six inches shorter than Carter, so he had to come all the way up on his toes to come close to Carter's ear with his lips.

"The lady at the bar . . . ?"

Carter nodded.

"Bildo, the muscle at the door, and two others just hustled her out through the back storage room."

Their heads shifted and Carter spoke in Dakin's ear using the same low tones. "Is that the room marked Private?"

"Yes. Another one is bringing a limo around from the garage."

Carter made a split-second decision. If he hadn't been sure before that something could be learned from the Navy commander's wife, he was sure of it now.

"I'm going after the woman. I'll need a car and a good driver."

"You've got it. A green BMW . . . it's parked directly across the street from the club. The driver's name is Stafford."

"Good. Give your men the signal. Come down on this place like the hounds from hell . . . employees, patrons, and anybody else connected with the club. Get 'em all in a net, and then squeeze."

Claude Dakin was a good man. He asked no questions, just nodded and scooted out the door.

Carter waited a three count, then followed. The door marked Private at the end of the hall was unlocked. He slid through it silently.

Before entering the club earlier he had shifted Wilhelmina's leather from under his left arm and secured the holster around his right leg. Now he pulled the Luger and moved through the floor-to-ceiling shelves toward a red light marked Exit.

Just before he reached the door, a tall figure appeared out of the near darkness at its side.

"Here now, sir, this is private back here. What can I do for—"

Carter brought the Luger's barrel up from his side and caught the man on the point of his chin. The surprised man staggered and fell back with a growl of pain.

His back hit the wall and Carter was right on him. This time the barrel caught him flush on the side of the neck, and Carter gave him a knee in the face on the way down.

Without another sound the man crumpled to the floor, and Carter made the door.

The rear alley was dark except for a streetlight to its right at its far end. A stretch black Rolls, its taillights gleaming like two red-eyed beacons, was just making the turn into another alley that would take it out to the street.

To Carter's left, two doors down from the Mainstem, was another narrow lane. He galloped to the corner, turned, and then sprinted toward the street.

The Rolls was just pulling out into traffic. Carter spotted two in the front and three in the rear. The ash blond head was clearly visible between the two men in the rear.

The green BMW was just where Dakin said it was.

Carter walked calmly toward it until he hit the passenger side door.

"Stafford?"

"Yes, sir."

"Can you make a U-turn here?"

He could and did, narrowly missing a taxi and two motor scooters.

"Good man. It's a black Rolls limo . . . that one about two blocks ahead."

"I saw it pull out, sir."

"Stay out of sight if you can, Stafford. Just in case, I'd like to know where they're taking her."

"Right-o, sir."

Stafford advanced and fell back like a pro, always keeping the Rolls's taillights in sight but never squeezing them.

It was still early enough that the traffic was heavy. That, coupled with the fact that the fog was starting to roll in, made detection by the driver of the Rolls that much more difficult.

"The driver's a foreigner, sir," Stafford said, breaking into Carter's thoughts.

"How so?"

"The way he makes his turns: too wide to the right, too short to the left."

"Any idea which way he's heading?"

"Not for certain," the man replied. "But I'll wager he's not leaving the city. He's bypassed the turns to the M23 and the M25, and he's already too far south for the M3 West."

Carter digested that and concentrated on the Rolls.

They left Charing Cross Road at Trafalgar Square and came out on Northumberland Avenue.

"They're turning left," Carter said.

"Yes, sir. Victoria Embankment."

They were near the Thames now, and the fog was getting heavier by the second. Also, the traffic was cut by at least two thirds.

"Can you douse your lights just before we make the turn?" Carter asked.

"Not very wise, sir."

Carter reluctantly accepted Stafford's judgment.

As they passed Cleopatra's Needle, Stafford slowed the car to a near idle. Ahead, the Rolls paused at the lights of Waterloo Bridge.

"If they go over the bridge to Southwark, sir, they're sure to spot our tail on Waterloo Road."

Carter nodded grimly. "Then we'll force them over and take her."

"Right-o, sir."

But the Rolls moved on through the intersection to the other part of Victoria Embankment. Just short of Blackfriars Bridge, they turned down the hill toward the Thames. In seconds the red lights were lost in the fog.

"Where does that go?"

"Under the bridge and along the Thames side of Blackfriars. I don't understand."

"Why?" Carter asked.

"That's Upper Thames Street beyond Blackfriars, sir. It's closed off after six o'clock this time of the year because of fog. It's a dead end."

"So where we are is the only way out?"

"Yes, unless . . ."

They both got it at the same time.

"Get on your radio, quick!" Carter barked. "See if you can get me a boat!"

"First Officer Stafford, Special Branch, to ALX . . ."

"ALX, the Yard, Gilley here . . . go ahead, Stafford."

"Have you a launch about tonight, Gilley?"

"We do . . . Captain Monroe in Y-26."

"Can you patch me through?"

"Can do . . ."

Ten seconds later a barrel-toned voice growled through the static.

"Monroe Y-26 here. What can I do for you, Special Branch?"

"What's your position?"

"Downstream from Custom House, just under Southwark Bridge."

"Tell him to hold his position until he hears from us again," Carter whispered.

Stafford relayed the message, and it was quickly acknowledged.

The BMW moved forward like a dark creeping ghost in the fog. Thirty feet above them yellow light glowed hazily from the lamps along the river, but very little of it reached the street.

Twice Stafford nearly nicked the sides of parked cars with the BMW's fender. Neither of them was the Rolls.

"There!" Carter said, pointing.

Stafford edged to the curb and parked. Carter slipped from the car and leaned back through the window.

"Have Monroe stand by."

Stafford nodded, and Carter slithered through the fog. He checked the Rolls. It was empty and locked. Just beyond it were steps leading down to what must have been the river. He couldn't see; he could only hear lapping water against the concrete embankment.

Other than the water's sound and foghorns up and down the river, there was total, eerie silence.

The steps were guarded by a low iron gate whose hinges had garnered at least a hundred years of rust.

Carter didn't chance it. He used the top of the seawall for a fulcrum and went over the gate.

Halfway down the steps he heard voices that brought him to a halt and made him fill his hand with Wilhelmina.

"She's passed out."

"All the better. The goddamned bitch nearly chewed off one of my fingers!"

Americans. Southern . . . Georgia or Alabama.

"Why don't we just drive down there?"

"It's better to bring her in from the river side. No one will see us in this fog."

"No one will see us again if we run under a ship!"

"Not a fear there, laddie. I know the Thames like me own bed. Now get aboard."

Seconds later, a powerful inboard marine engine sputtered and roared to life.

Carter moved forward in a crouch until he ran out of steps. Through the murky fingers of fog he could see pilings and several small boats bobbing at their lines.

A broad cement facing ran along the seawall. He followed this toward the sound of the engine and then spotted it.

It was a powerful, Packard-powered ex-RAF rescue launch. Carter could already see water churning off its stern from the twin props.

As the launch eased around and began to idle out between the piers and other moored boats, Carter fell to his belly. He crawled to the very end of the cement and strained his eyes toward the boat's stern.

He could see huddled figures, and a darkly clad man in a turtleneck sweater and black ducks was at the wheel. But he couldn't make out the launch's markings.

When the boat was lost in the fog, Carter jumped to his feet and ran back up the stairs. Once back over the gate, he pounded toward the BMW.

"Tell this Monroe what he needs to know as quickly as possible. I'll give him the rest when I'm on board. They said 'down,' so I'm assuming they're heading toward Westminster."

Stafford did as he was told in clipped, rapid-fire sentences.

Captain Monroe's voice came back the same way. "Tell your man I'll pick him up at Scott's *Discovery*, 109."

"Roger."

"You know that?" Carter asked, folding himself into the car.

"I know it," Stafford said, wheeling the BMW around and slamming a suctioned blue light onto the roof. "They've secured the Mainstem. Everyone who was inside is on the way to the Yard."

"Fantastic," Carter growled, sure now that he needed Mrs. Pearson to find the link they must have, but hoping that something from the Mainstem raid would add to it.

"They found a shortwave in one of the upstairs offices."

Carter felt a cold chill seep up his spine. "Anyone get a chance to use it?"

"Negative, but the big man, Adamo, tried."

"And . . . ?"

"He's dead."

Fanatics, Carter thought. *They're all fanatics*.

EIGHT

The Customs launch was a chugger, thirty feet of underpowered, broad-beamed marine antiquity.

But Carter soon found out that high-speed chases were a rarity on the Thames. This did away with the need for speed, and Captain Monroe did the rest. It was as if he and his three crewmen had eyes that could pierce the fog.

"One of those sixty-knot-an-hour skimmers, huh?" he had said, reacting to Carter's words soon after AXE's finest had jumped on board.

"I'm sure of it."

"Well, he'll not have much chance to use all those horses tonight. Visibility's down, maybe ten meters. Worse yet, there's traffic . . . lots of it."

They had moved a third of the way into the wide part of the Thames, and now they were idling along with the foghorn blasting their presence every now and then.

Carter knew that for many men the Thames was as familiar in sunlight as the back of their hands. But in the fog it was a mysterious wasteland.

Not so for Captain Monroe and his helmsman.

Almost from the second they heard the roar of the big Packard engines, they had honed in on the JOUST launch as if the old Customs boat had every ounce of radar equipment on board that money could buy.

Ahead of them the bow split the thick mist, allowing them to see the ten or so meters Monroe had claimed. Behind them, the fog closed in to become a gray-white wall.

"Where are we?" Carter asked.

"Just off Westminster. That'll be the Houses of Parliament off to our starboard there."

Carter peered to the right. He would have to take the captain's word for it. He couldn't see a damned thing.

Other than engine sounds, it seemed that there were a hundred foghorns on the river.

At their crawling speed, the boat rocked in the water. This was made worse nearer to the river's center, where the water was choppier and the current swifter.

"What'd these blokes do?" Monroe asked, his head cocked to the side listening for the now familiar growl of the Packard engines. "Steal the Crown Jewels?"

"Not exactly," Carter replied, "but possibly as valuable. They said something about landing and bringing her in from the river side. Are there private piers along here for homes?"

"Used to be," Monroe replied, "about two hundred and fifty years ago. That was before the embankments were built. Now the only places like that would be way west and south of Battersea, far outside the city."

"I think that may be where they're going."

"Then they'll have a long ride tonight."

"He must be finding his way through the traffic," Carter said, hearing the Packard idle back, only to roar to life again.

"Aye, he may not know the river too well, but he knows his horns. Not all of them are boats, and you got to know which is which. Hear that?"

A particularly low, mournful wail rolled across the water, and Carter nodded.

"That's Lambeth Bridge. We'll be coming up on it shortly. He slowed for it and then just sailed through. He knows his horns."

Suddenly the rusted side of a large boat—one about ten times the size of the Customs launch—glided by the port side.

Carter gripped the roof of the wheelhouse until his knuckles were white.

The other boat had missed them by less than ten feet.

The lanky young helmsman saw the white line along Carter's jaw and threw him a boyish grin. "I heard him."

"I'm glad," Carter replied.

The minutes dragged by. A half hour passed, and then an hour.

"Cut to idle," Captain Monroe said, his hand falling on the young helmsman's shoulder.

"Aye, sir."

The old diesel idled down as all hands sharpened their ears to the various sounds rolling toward them through the thick mist.

"I don't hear him . . ." Carter said.

"Shhh," Monroe hissed, moving his hand to Carter's shoulder and squeezing.

The boat rocked gently. And then Carter heard it too. It was no longer a roar, but a low, steady hum.

"They're docking," Monroe said, "somewhere off to port. Up to one third."

Carter stared over the wheelhouse off the port bow as the young sailor brought his speed up and turned the bow into the current. They ran less than a minute before Monroe spoke again.

"We've passed 'em. Bring her about, lad, to starboard."

"Ayc, sir."

The old Customs launch heaved about, its port side bucking the current, and then they were picking up speed.

"Reverse . . . idle," Monroe barked.

Carter felt the vibration as the screw reversed. Then they were still moving with the current but at a snail's pace.

"Where do ya make us, lad?"

"Past Battersea Park Road, sir. We may be near halfway to Epsom."

Monroe turned to Carter. "There'll be yer houses along here where they could land."

Carter chewed his lip for a moment and then asked, "Is there any way I can find out which house . . . without alarming them?"

Monroe turned to the stern. "Ready the small boat, lads, and rig a lifeline." Then he turned back to the helmsman. "Make another run, lad, and bring her to starboard twenty meters."

When the bigger boat had come around again, closer to shore and upstream, the dinghy was launched. In seconds it disappeared in the fog with both sailors rowing frantically, more to ride the current than for speed.

In no time the line attached to the small craft was tugged three times.

"Lend a hand here, sir," Monroe whispered. "Let's heave the lads back in."

Carter and the captain pulled at the line hand over hand. Evidently the two seamen had done the same, for they quickly burst out of the fog and clambered aboard, tugging the rubber boat on deck behind them.

" 'Bout right, sir. Epsom Road pier's about a mile off." He pointed over the stern.

"And the launch?" Carter asked.

"She's partially under cover, but we spotted her. It's a big house with . . ."

"Sir?"

Carter turned to the younger of the two sailors, a slight young man of about nineteen with freckles dotting his whole face. "Yes?"

"I know the house, sir. Grew up in Epsom, I did. Did gardening work fer all the lordies along here when I was a tad. This place belongs to an MP, it does . . . Thomas Carstairs-Wright."

Carter stared hard at the sailor. "Describe it to me, son . . . every detail you can remember."

The young man had an excellent memory. By the time he was finished, Carter had a pretty good floor plan of the house and grounds in his mind.

"You goin' in there alone, are ya, sir?" Monroe asked.

Carter nodded.

He had already toyed with the idea of radioing MI5 for backup and dismissed it.

It was pretty obvious that Elise Pearson knew too much

for her own good, whether she knew it or not. Twenty agents descending on the Carstairs-Wright house in the middle of the night might be an open invitation to have her killed.

Carter had already seen the kamikazelike reaction of Admiral Number One's troops in a given situation.

"Is there somewhere nearby where you can land me?"

Monroe looked at the young sailor, who nodded.

"There's a walk-up over the seawall right beside Epsom Road. We could take ya in with the rubber boat."

"Then let's do it," Carter said, turning to the helmsman. "Have you got another cap and black sweater like you're wearing?"

"Aye, sir."

"Break 'em out!"

"Blimey," came the reply, "it's just like a bleedin' commando raid!"

Killmaster N3 just smiled.

The sailor didn't know how right he was.

Two cars and a motorcycle passed Carter in the fog, forcing him into the trees that lined the narrow lane.

He jogged the full mile from Epsom Road back toward the Carstairs-Wright house. When the terrain began to resemble the boy's description, he slowed to a walk and remained in the shadows of the roadside trees.

The fog here was only half as thick as it had been on the river, but clear vision was still less than a hundred yards.

The houses were really estates, with high walls and heavy woods obscuring them from the road. Each had a frontage of about two hundred yards and a depth, from the road to the river, of at least twice that.

The lights of each house, as Carter passed, seemed eerie, almost macabre, sifting to him through the thick trees made thicker with heavy gray fingers of fog.

"Third from the bend," the sailor had said. "Ya can't miss it 'cause the gate's new, made of steel. All the other places have the old iron grillwork in front. Also, the Carstairs-Wright place is the only one with a brick wall.

The others is stone. An' it's a high one. Ya'll need a line, ya will, sir."

The young man had been right.

The wall above him was at least twice his height if not a foot more. Also, the trees and shrubbery had been cut away from it to form at least a twelve-foot clearance.

He crossed the road into heavier trees and approached the gate from their cover. When he could see through the steel bars to the winding lane beyond, he dropped to his belly to assess the situation.

The gate was the only way. The wall was impossible to scale, and there were no trees close enough to swing over.

Carter uncoiled the line from his shoulder and made a lariat knot. When it was ready, he threaded the end of the line and shook out the loop.

He was just about to stand, when from beyond the gate he heard a booted foot on gravel. Seconds later a figure sidled from behind the wall and stopped at the center of the gate.

The figure wore a khaki shirt and trousers tucked into jump boots, and slung over his shoulder was a Browning 20-gauge 5-plug shotgun. Even in the fog Carter could see that several inches of the Browning's barrel had been sawed off.

It wasn't a whole lot of firepower, but up close it could make one hell of a mess out of anything it hit.

The guy peered through the bars so intently and for such a length of time that, for a moment, Carter thought he had been spotted.

Carter fingered the butt of the Luger under his left armpit and then decided against it. He could drop the guy easily from this distance, effectively and silently, but the clock on the man's belt made the difference.

He probably keyed in every twenty minutes or so. If someone in the house didn't record it, they would come looking for the shirker.

A full five minutes passed, and then Carter heard the reason for the guard's presence: the low hum of a powerful engine in the distance. It grew steadily louder, and then, from his left, came the light from a pair of yellow fog beams.

The guard was already unlocking the gates and swinging them wide as the car glided into view in the lane. It was a four-door Jag sedan, coal black and, from the sound of the engine, supercharged.

Carter held his breath as the car rocked to a halt at the gate, dust billowing up all around it.

The guard approached with a flash.

Using the sound of the Jaguar's engine to cover his movement, Carter sidestepped through the trees until he could get a clear view of the side of the car.

It was a summit meeting.

The driver's face was bathed in bandages. It wasn't hard—from the placement of the bandages and the guy's hair and size—to figure that he was the one who had wasted Bridgit Michaels. Beside him was the short, bespectacled man with the receding hairline.

Carter had already made him once driving another Jaguar: Harley Donne.

On Carter's side, in the back seat, was Lady Lenore Grayburn herself. She was wearing a wig and dark glasses, but there was no mistaking that profile.

Beside Lady Grayburn in the back seat was another passenger, a male, but Carter couldn't get a reading on him.

It was too much to hope that he might be the admiral himself.

The guard touched his fingers to his forehead, and the Jaguar moved, leaving another cloud of dust. The guard was close behind it, and in no time the gates were once more closed and locked.

To Carter's relief, instead of moving along the inside of the wall, the guard moved up the twisting lane the Jaguar had just taken.

That didn't mean that there weren't more guards with sawed-off shotguns on the perimeter of the grounds, but at least this one was gone. More than likely he had killed two birds with one trip: allowed the Jag's entrance and checked his perimeter at the same time.

With any luck he would now be heading for coffee.

Carter moved across the road, playing cowboy as he ran, with the loop of the line curling in lazy circles over his head.

Halfway there, he tossed it. The guard passed out of sight around a turn in the lane just as the line settled around two spikes atop the gate. Carter drew it taut. By the time he reached the gate he didn't even have to pause in the momentum of his run.

He walked, hand over hand, right up the steel rungs until he could pull himself to the side and on top of the wall. Once there, he undid the loop and used both ends of the rope to lower himself down the other side.

When his feet hit the dirt, he pulled the line down after him and quickly hid it in a patch of thick shrubbery.

Like a shadow he moved up the lane. Beyond the trees were formal gardens, complete with graveled paths, low hedges, and ornate fountains. Staying off the paths and in the heaviest patches of fog he could find, Carter moved toward the side of the old mansion.

The four stories of the house looked far less sinister up close, with lights blazing in most of the windows.

Along the side of the mansion, just before the hill slanted down toward the river, were several carports. Here the lane made a U-turn in a wide arc.

Three of the carports were occupied: the Jaguar sedan he had just seen arrive; a Ford Cortina; and the little Jag roadster Harley Donne had used to escape from Grayburn House and Cardiff.

One by one, quietly easing open their doors, Carter checked for keys. He came up dry on both Jags, but it was bingo at the Cortina.

Pocketing the keys, still using the foggy darkness as a shield, he moved on through the carport and down the hill. At the rear corner of the house he found more gardens.

Unlike the front of the mansion with its blazing windows, only three had lights in the rear: two on the ground floor and one on the fourth.

A boxwood hedge ran the length of the rear wall, pausing only at a jutting veranda and then continuing again.

With any luck—and if the youthful sailor's memory was running true to form—he would never make the veranda.

He didn't.

About thirty feet from the corner was a dark stairwell. Carter came up on it so suddenly he almost fell down the stairs.

The door at the bottom was locked by an old and rusty padlock. Hugo made short work of it, and then Carter ran his fingers over the hinges.

Just as he thought, they were as rusty as the padlock.

Back up the stairs and into the hedge he went.

It took him nearly two minutes to find what he wanted by feel alone: milkweed. Several of the gummy-centered plants grew along the base of the hedge that faced the sun.

He cut two large handfuls and retraced his steps to the door. One handful he squeezed over both hinges, then he worked it in with his fingers. He did the second handful the same way as he carefully and very slowly eased the door back and forth.

The gummy juice from the milkweed stems did its job. In no time Carter was able to open the door enough to squeeze through. The hinges made no squeak of protest as he closed the door behind him.

He played the beam of his penlight over the wine racks until it found an old, wooden stairwell. At the top was a door that, from the hinges, Carter knew opened into the wine cellar.

That was a plus. Now if only the door wasn't locked.

It wasn't.

Beyond it was a small room that doubled as a broom closet and pantry. At the other end was another door. This one had four panes that allowed Carter to see into a mammoth kitchen.

The young seaman had been absolutely correct about every exterior detail of the house, the wine cellar, and the kitchen. Because of that, Carter was inside.

Now he was on his own.

Every light in the kitchen blazed, and the aromas of food wafted through the door to Carter's nostrils. The sound of low voices also reached him from a room off the kitchen.

Then the voices grew louder, and a man and woman wearing the uniforms of household servants entered. They were closely followed by Lenore Grayburn.

The blond wig was gone now, and her sleek black hair fell in cascading waves to her bare shoulders.

Carter had to admit it; she was magnificent.

She wore a full-length evening gown. And what a gown. It was a black crêpe sheath with a wide scooped neck tickled with lace that left most of her shoulders bare and revealed a good three inches of tight cleavage between the bulging mounds of her breasts.

The dress had a lot of class as well as creating a great deal of anticipation in the viewer. It looked like one deep breath and La Grayburn would be walking around naked to the waist.

Carter moved closer to the door but stayed in the shadows.

Lady Grayburn was giving the servants instructions about dinner.

Jesus, Carter thought, *they're about ready to blow up the world and they take time out for a formal dinner party!*

"As soon as Mr. Carstairs-Wright arrives, you may serve. That should be in about thirty minutes. In the meantime, Harold, will you be so good as to serve the others another cocktail in the den?"

The butler nodded and left.

"Annie, please prepare a tray for our guest."

"Yes, mum."

"Put it in the lift, and I'll take it to her myself."

"Yes, mum."

Carter almost sighed aloud with relief. The unknown was now known—or at least he could hope. The "guest" might not be Elise Pearson, but the odds were in Carter's favor that it was. Read "guest" as a "prisoner" who would not be coming down to dinner, and it almost had to come up Elise.

As the maid set about preparing the tray, Lenore Grayburn came dangerously close to the door.

Carter moved back in to the shadows and watched her pour a glass of wine from the sideboard.

Up close her face was both chilling and beautiful. She had high cheekbones, and the angles of her face were so severe that it gave her an exotic, almost Oriental look. There was no doubt that the face fit the body: exciting.

But it was also strained and the eyes were restless. Every movement, even raising the glass of wine to her glossed lips, was agitated and nervous.

Then it hit Carter.

She was sultry, even sexy. But there was nothing feminine about her.

"Ready, mum."

"Thank you, Annie."

She placed her own glass of wine on the tray and moved past the maid to an open cupboard filled with canned goods.

"I'll go up the back stairs."

"Very well, mum."

Shades of "Upstairs, Downstairs," Carter thought as he watched the cupboard swing open to reveal a narrow set of carpeted stairs.

Lenore Grayburn moved up the stairs, leaving the cupboard open behind her. The maid slid open a small door nearby and pushed the tray into the dumbwaiter.

"Annie . . . ?"

"Yes, sir?"

It was Bandage Face. The top half of him leaned through the arch into the kitchen.

"Any more olives out here?"

"Yes, sir. I'll bring them, sir."

He disappeared, and the maid closed the cupboard door. From a shelf she selected a bottle and then she was gone.

Carter wasted no time. He slipped into the kitchen, darted across, and opened the cupboard just wide enough to sidle into the passageway. With the door closed behind him, he scanned the stairs upward.

They were thinly carpeted with a narrow runner and illuminated every few feet by a low-watt yellow bulb. From somewhere above him he could hear the racket of Lenore Grayburn's pumps tap, tap, tapping her ascent.

Then he checked himself: black woolen turtleneck, tuxedo trousers . . . and shiny black leather shoes with very hard leather soles and heels.

Just what the well-dressed commando should wear.

Except for the shoes.

He would sound like an elephant going up those stairs, no matter how lightly he trod.

Quickly he removed them, tied the laces, and draped them around his neck.

This was barely done when he heard the grinding sound of the dumbwaiter being raised from somewhere on the other side of the wall.

Step by step Carter followed the sound up. When the maid grew tired of pulling and paused to rest, Carter paused.

Once past the third landing, he stopped altogether and attuned his ears to any sound from above.

The seconds crawled by as the dumbwaiter kept creeping upward, it seemed an inch at a time.

And then it stopped, and Carter heard the fourth-floor door grind open. When he heard once again the tapping of the woman's heels, he took the steps three at a time until just his forehead and eyes could see over the landing.

The hall looked longer than a football field and nearly as wide.

One quick look was all it took to see where the tray was going.

The ton of muscle from the club, Bildo, was sitting in a chair between the last door on the left of the hall and a pair of French doors at its end. A small semicircle of balcony was visible beyond the doors.

As Lady Grayburn approached, Bildo stood and flipped the cigarette he had been smoking out the opened half of the French doors. From his tuxedo pocket he produced a ring of keys and went to work on the door.

Carter's mind was moving like a jet, trying to figure some way of getting across the hall and into a room while the big bouncer's back was turned.

And then he didn't have to.

Bildo opened the door, Grayburn entered, and he entered right after her, closing the door behind him.

"Son of a bitch . . ."

The rest of the oath was muffled by the closing door, but what Carter heard brought a smile to his face.

Elise Pearson was very much alive and, from the thunder in her voice, very much awake.

Carter hit the landing in a dead run and didn't pause until he was through the French doors and out on the balcony.

One lightning-fast scan gave him the picture.

There was a narrow, four-inch ledge of concrete floor reinforcement running around every floor, about four feet beneath the window casements. Besides this, ivy and bougainvillea vines grew from the ground clear up to the rainspouts on the roof.

Carter checked them and found nearly every stalk as fat as his wrist.

Any given vine would support three men, let alone one.

Carter found the ledge with one set of toes, curled his fingers in the vines, and lifted off the balcony. Being careful to test each handhold before he moved, he crabwalked the twenty-odd feet to the lighted window.

He could hear Elise Pearson's voice blasting through the closed window as if it were open.

"I don't give a damn if the cause is worth any sacrifice! *You* sacrifice . . . not me!"

Lenore Grayburn said something in a lower tone Carter didn't catch, and then the prisoner's soprano again shattered the air.

"When I get out of here, I'll have every one of you

doing life! Now give me my clothes!"

There was another muted reply from Lady Grayburn, and Carter heard the door open and close through the French doors.

"Bring her down after Carstairs-Wright leaves," Grayburn said.

"Yes, madam."

"I'll have Harold dig a grave in the garden."

"Yes, madam."

Tap, tap, tap, and Grayburn was gone.

Sweat gushed from every pore in Carter's body as he, as quietly as possible, flattened himself against the vine-covered wall.

He heard, rather than saw, the giant light a cigarette and stand there on the little balcony humming a tuneless song.

It seemed an eternity before the guard flipped the butt into the fog and stepped back into the hall.

Grabbing a lower handhold on the vines, Carter pulled himself to the window and looked in.

The bed was bare, there were no drapes at the windows, and even the rug had been taken up from the floor.

And standing in the center of the room, fuming, her arms folded beneath her heaving breasts, was Elise Pearson.

She was stark naked.

NINE

Carter's next move was highly debatable.

If he slid the window open and dropped into the room out of nowhere, what would the woman do?

He guessed that, with her highly volatile temper and her usual vocal response, she would have Bildo in the room in seconds with her screaming.

On the other hand, if he signaled her through the window, her response to his presence could be just as loud and equally as dangerous.

He waited and watched.

With all of her bravado, it was pretty obvious that Elise Pearson was a very frightened woman. She displayed it in the way she paced, wringing her hands and chewing her lower lip in the process.

Once she came extremely close to the window in her pacing. As she stared pensively out at the fog and the night, Carter was tempted to take his chances and make his move.

But still he waited.

She was lovely, tall and straight with long tapering legs and high, full breasts. Her shining, shoulder-length hair softened her scowling features and its ash blond color accented her flashing green eyes.

Physically she was on a par with Lenore Grayburn.

But she was more.

Even through the window Carter could sense that, underneath her brash exterior and surface gloss, there was a real volcano of a woman.

Suddenly she moved away, across the room, this time with intent and purpose.

Carter held his breath until he was sure of her destination.

When the bathroom door closed behind her, he moved. The window slid up easily, and Carter dropped soundlessly to the floor inside, closing it behind him.

He positioned himself flat against the wall between the bed and bath. When he heard the commode flush, he tensed and lifted his arms high above his head.

When the door opened, Elise moved back into the room with the same pacing stride, hands wringing in front of her, head lowered in thought.

She was too shocked to scream when Carter dropped his left arm around her like a vise. He pinned both her arms and brought her body tightly up against his. At the same time, he clamped his hand over her mouth and nose and, heels dragging, tugged her back into the bath.

Just as he kicked the door shut behind them she came to her senses. She was a big woman and more than a handful. She fought like a tiger, and it was all Carter could do to keep her pinned to him until he could get his lips close to her ear.

"I'm not one of them."

A little less fight.

"I'm here to help you."

The body relaxed slightly, but not all the way. Carter sensed that the lady was still coiled to spring. She mumbled something, and he spoke again.

"If I take my hand away, do you agree to keep your mouth shut until I can explain? Nod!"

The nod was perfunctory, but it was there.

Just in case she decided to squeal after, Carter flushed the commode with his foot. The sound of the rushing water would muffle at least some of the sound.

The instant his arms released her, Elise whirled, her body tensed, her eyes flashing.

"You . . ."

"Me," Carter nodded, and then he reverted to the clipped accent he had used at their first meeting. "Cedric Dobbins here, at your service, mum."

"Bullshit!"

She still had some fire, Carter thought, and smiled.

"You're right. My name is Nick Carter. I'm an agent of the United States government."

"I hope you're a good one," Elise said, all the tenseness flowing from her body now, and a look of relief filling her lovely features.

"I am," Carter said, opening the bathroom door a crack to make sure her keeper hadn't gotten wary.

"Would you please tell me what the hell is going on?" she cried.

"Keep your voice down."

"All right. What's going on?"

"How much do you know about your husband's activities?"

"Ha," she said with a short laugh, "less than nothing! We have a very loose marriage . . . in that I haven't seen him in almost a year!"

"That would figure," Carter said, turning back to face her.

Her eyebrows raised sharply. "You mean Ralph has something to do with this?"

"Lady, he has one hell of a lot to do with it."

Carter checked the bath. They had stripped that, too; no towels, no bathmat, even the shower curtain was missing.

Elise followed his gaze. "What are you looking for?"

"Something for you to wear," he replied.

Only then did she apparently realize that she had been carrying on a conversation with a perfect stranger for three minutes in the nude.

She crossed one arm over her breasts. One hand did a poor job of trying to conceal the triangle at her thighs.

Carter looked and shrugged.

She looked and did the same.

"What the hell." She gave it up and looked Carter

directly in the eye. "What do we do now?"

"Try to get the hell out of here."

She digested that for a moment and seemed to make a decision. "How do I know that if I go with you I'm not going from the frying pan into the fire?"

"You don't. But you don't have much choice."

Carter was pulling off the heavy black turtleneck. He still wore the frilled-front tuxedo shirt beneath it.

"Here, put this on!"

She did.

It came just low enough and would do for the time being.

"What's the matter?" she asked, seeing his lips curl into a smile.

"Nothing. It's just odd that you're even more sexy in the turtleneck than nude."

Carter didn't think it was possible to make Elise Pearson blush. He was wrong. But she quickly overcame it and got back to the matter at hand.

"Why have they brought me here?"

"I don't know," Carter replied, "and I won't know until I can get you to a place where we can talk in peace and I can pick your brains."

"It is Ralph, isn't it?"

Carter nodded. "He's part of a group called JOUST."

A cloud—tiny but still there—passed over Elise's eyes. Its presence told Carter that she did know something.

"You've heard of them, haven't you?"

"Kind of . . . by the back door, so to speak. But I don't know what they're all about, or where I fit in."

"Suffice it to say you know more than you think you do. In fact, enough to get you killed."

"Ridiculous!"

"Oh, yeah? Listen, lady, right now the butler is somewhere in the backyard digging your grave."

Her face went chalk white.

Carter knew from that point on she would do exactly as she was told.

• • •

Nick Carter stood on the rim of the tub, one hand holding on to the shower curtain rod for balance. His other hand was full of 9mm Luger.

"What's that?" Elise had asked when he had pulled the long, ugly silencer from its special niche in Wilhelmina's holster.

"It's a silencer," he replied, attaching it to the Luger's barrel.

"You mean, you're—"

"Yeah," he said, cutting her off. "You just do what I told you to do, and don't watch."

"Jesus, this is for keeps, isn't it?"

"Yes, it is."

The commode was running full blast now, overflowing because of a full roll of paper Carter had stuffed in it a few minutes earlier.

"You ready?" Elise asked in a low voice from just around the door.

"Ready," Carter whispered. "Do it!"

He heard her bare feet pad across the bare parquet floor and then her knuckles rap lightly on the door.

"Yeah?" came Bildo's muffled query.

"You can take the tray. I'm finished."

"The maid will get it later."

"I got another problem."

"What the hell is it?"

"The john's overflowing. It's running all over the place."

"Christ."

Keys jangled, and then Carter heard the door being opened.

"Step back!"

The door closed and Carter heard the big man relock it.

"What happened?" he growled.

"How do I know?" Elise snapped. "I'm not a plumber!"

"I'll take a look."

Carter narrowed his eyes. Wilhelmina's safety was off. A steel-jacketed hollow-point was resting in the chamber.

He traced Bildo across the room by the sound of his footsteps.

Carter had no choice. It had to be this way. He couldn't afford a hand-to-hand with the big bouncer. The noise would surely bring half the people down below bounding up the stairs.

It had to be done quickly, quietly . . . and permanently.

"Goddamnit, it's runnin' all over the place!"

"I told you."

Carter could see him through the narrow crack below the door's top hinge. His concentration was riveted on the water seeping out into the bedroom.

He moved through the door. Carter saw his hand, his arm, then his head and shoulders. He bent to lift the commode seat, and Carter leaned forward.

The snout of the silencer was two inches from his left ear when Carter fired.

The thud of the slug entering his ear and jarring his brain made more noise than the explosion of the shell.

The power, at such close range, was that of a cannon. Somewhere inside his head the slug spread out. When it exited, half the man's brain came with it, making a mess of the bathroom wall.

Carter dropped to the wet floor behind the fallen body and retrieved the ring of keys where they had fallen. Then he stepped into the bedroom, closing the door behind him.

Elise stood, her hands over her stomach, her eyes like silver dollars on the closed door.

"I told you not to watch."

"God, you . . . you blew his head off." She was starting to shake.

Carter retrieved the turtleneck from beneath the bed. He tugged it over her head, and when her eyes emerged through the neck hole, they were wild.

"Who are you?"

"You really mean, what kind of a man am I, don't you?"

"Yes."

"The kind who can slap you silly if you get hysterical on me. Now come on!"

The third key opened the door. Carter quickly checked the hall, then glanced back at her over his shoulder.

"Stay here!"

He moved down the hall, listening at each door before opening it and peering inside.

The third door he tried was the one.

A closet door stood open, and beyond it women's clothing rested neatly on a line of hangers.

One minute later he was back with a pair of slacks and a pair of low-heeled pumps.

"Put these on, quick!"

Like a glazed automaton, Elise Pearson followed his command. His guess had been close to perfect. Elise and Lenore Grayburn were nearly the same size all over. Even the shoes were only half a size off.

Carter locked the door, removed that particular key from the ring, and threw it as far as he could into the night.

"Stay close!" he hissed.

She did, literally curling her fingers into the back of his belt, all the way down the hall and the stairs.

At the bottom of the narrow staircase, Carter eased the cupboard door open just a crack.

It looked as though a few courses of dinner had already been served and they were down to the entree. A huge roast on a silver platter was sitting on the butcher block table in the center of the room.

Both the maid and the butler kept popping in and out of the kitchen. There were seconds when the room was empty, but the chances were too great to make the dash across to the wine cellar door.

The minutes dragged by, and Carter knew that every one counted.

"I'll slice a few pieces off for the one upstairs and take it up to him while you serve."

The butler nodded.

Sweat beaded and trickled off Carter's chin.

If the maid took Bildo's dinner up these stairs, they were dead.

And then he saw it . . . about a foot over his head in a standing position.

A fuse box.

Thank God for proper English households, he thought, running his fingers down the very precise labeling beside each fuse.

When he had located "Kitchen," he crouched back down beside Elise.

"Are you cool now?" he whispered.

"Yes."

"Are you sure?"

"Yes, damnit!"

"Okay. This is a cupboard door. Directly across from it is the door to a pantry room. It's about twenty-five feet, and the door opens toward you, with the knob on the left-hand side."

She looked perplexed.

"I'm telling you all this because we're going to have to cross the kitchen and get into that pantry in the dark."

Her eyes widened for just an instant, then she nodded firmly. "I've got it."

"Good. Run with your hands out in front of you. There's nothing in your way until you get to the door."

"Right."

Carter took another look into the kitchen. The butler was gone. The maid was cutting the roast and preparing a plate.

Carter stood and placed his thumb and index finger on the fuse.

"Ready?"

"As I'll ever be," Elise said and gulped.

Carter twisted the fuse, plunging the kitchen into total darkness. A split second later he shoved the door and dropped his hand on Elise's shoulder as a signal to go.

He gave her a solid three count, and took off behind her.

"Harold . . . Harold, we've blown a bloody fuse!"

Just inside the pantry, Carter crashed into Elise but managed to keep both their bodies upright. He closed the first door behind them and felt with his hands until he found her head.

"There's another door into the wine cellar," he whispered, his lips flat against her ear. "Put your arm around me!"

She did, and Carter moved them, side by side, a few steps down the stairs. When that door was safely shut behind them, he snapped on the penlight and kept moving.

He was glad to see that she followed without being told. She was functioning again on all eight, and Carter sensed that from here on in he could count on Elise to hold up her end.

At the outside door he paused only long enough to replace his shoes before moving out.

At the corner of the house he explained briefly the next part of his plan and how he planned to pull it off.

Elise nodded her understanding at practically every word.

"Can you drive?"

"Anything short of Formula One," she quipped.

"It's a four-speed Cortina. C'mon!"

At the carports he paused, grabbing her arm.

The little Jag roadster and the Cortina still sat in the same places he had found them. The big Jag sedan was gone.

And then he remembered Lady Grayburn's instructions to the maid: "As soon as Mr. Carstairs-Wright arrives, you may serve. That should be in about thirty minutes."

From the looks of it, Mr. Carstairs-Wright had been fairly close by. Close enough for someone to take the Jag sedan and go get him.

"Wait here!"

Before she could ask why, Carter was off at a crouched jog toward the front corner of the house.

Sure enough. The Jag sedan was parked in the other

circular drive, the one that went in front of the mansion's main entrance. Idly he wondered if the driver had left the keys in that powerful machine. He would dearly love to get out of there with that supercharger beneath his foot. But the gleaming lights from the front windows discouraged him from making the cross to the sedan and checking.

He moved back to the rear of the Cortina and motioned Elise out of the shadows.

"You push as much as you can from the driver's side. When it's rolling, hop in. When it's rolling good, flip the key on with the clutch in and drop it into second."

"I told you . . . I know how to drive."

"So you did," he said, giving her shoulder a squeeze. "But don't drop the clutch until we're almost at the gate. From that distance they might not hear it from the house."

"What about the gate?"

"We ram it."

"What? With a Cortina?"

"Don't worry about it. The gate opens out. It's designed to keep people out . . . not in. If you hit it hard, the two sides will buckle out and the gates will pop open."

She chuckled. "You sound as if you've done this sort of thing before."

Carter matched her chuckle. "There's not much I haven't done before. Move!"

The first few feet were hell. There was a slight rise at the opening of the carport, and it took all the strength both of them possessed to get the car rolling back and forth until finally it slid over the concrete bump.

"Get in!" Carter hissed, still pushing with all his might.

He heard, rather than saw, Elise jump into the car. The door clicked shut behind her, and then the Cortina hit the downhill slope. In seconds it was rolling, picking up speed much faster than Carter had expected.

He had to hustle like hell to catch up to the passenger side door, yank it open, and jump in.

"Set?"

"Yeah," she replied, only a quiver of fear in her voice. "All the way."

They were clipping along at a good rate when they hit the first of the two curves in the long lane. Just around it, Carter froze.

"Shit . . ."

In front of them, just rounding the second curve, were two guards, and they weren't slow on the uptake. One and one equaled two . . . rolling Cortina with engine dead and lights off equaled something very wrong.

They stopped dead center in the middle of the lane, both of them swinging their sawed-off shotguns down into firing position from their shoulders.

"Drop the clutch!"

She responded, and the Cortina's engine roared into life.

"Floor it!" Nothing. "Damnit, floor it!"

He looked over. She was frozen. She could do all commands except the big one . . . kill.

The two guards were aiming now. Carter could almost see the gleam in their eyes over the short barrels of the shotguns.

He slid his own rear end off the seat until it thudded on the floor and with his left arm pulled her flat to the seat, yanking her foot off the accelerator. At the same time, he found it with his own foot and grasped the steering wheel with his right hand.

He mashed the pedal, and the little car jumped ahead as if it had been goosed. Taking his bearings through the windshield off the trees above them, Carter steered in the middle of the lane directly, he hoped, for the two men.

And then all hell broke loose at the same time.

They fired. The windshield shattered, sending glass fragments across both their bodies. Seconds later Carter heard a solid thud, quickly followed by a scream of pain.

He was hoping for the second thud, but it never came.

"Move," he cried, "out of the way!"

She scooted across the seat, and Carter, his foot still on the floor, hoisted himself upright.

He used Wilhelmina to mash out what was left of the windshield and righted the car. In the side rearview mirror he could see number two running wildly down the lane behind them, reloading the shotgun as he came.

"Brace yourself," Carter growled as the steel gates hurtled toward them.

The night erupted with the agonizing sound of smashing glass and tearing metal. Elise had braced herself, but it still wasn't good enough. The crash threw her to the floor. Carter's chest hit the steering wheel, but he was able to cushion the shock somewhat with his hands and forearms.

When he looked up, another expletive slid from his lips.

The center of the gate yawned only partially open. The front of the Cortina, Carter knew, was a mess, but the gates had held. It was only by a thread of the lock, but it was enough to make them have another run at it before the gates would give entirely.

The guard was thirty yards behind them, coming at a dead run and leveling the shotgun as he came.

Carter hit reverse, floored the Cortina, and dropped the clutch.

The tires screamed in protest, but they caught and the car hurtled backward, the front fishtailing.

"Stay down!" Carter screamed, seeing Elise's bewildered face out of the corner of his eye.

The shotgun roared just before the back of the Cortina caught him in the knees. He went up and over Carter's side of the car, landing near the trees beside the lane.

He was game and a pro. He had barely lit before he rolled to his belly, bringing the gun up to use the second barrel. His face was a contorted mask of both fury and agony, and blood was spurting from both his nostrils, but he was still determined to shoot.

Carter leveled Wilhelmina over the door and pumped two slugs into the top of his head.

He didn't know what they did and he didn't care. The guy was dead; that was all that was important.

He hit the gates in second, doing about thirty-five, and they were through.

TEN

Nick Carter knew this part of the countryside to the southwest of London fairly well. In no time he found Castlebar Road and had the Cortina growling at fifty-five.

"You all right?"

"Fine . . . now," Elise replied, crawling up onto the seat.

Carter checked her out from the corner of his eye. She was. The wind, through what was left of that side of the windshield, was blowing her fine blond hair straight back from her head. Her features were screwed into a look of solid determination.

"Sorry I froze back there. I . . . I've never killed anybody before."

"It's always hard the first time."

"Do you always have to be so goddamned flip?"

"Not always, just most of the time."

Carter force-fed the mid-sized car, making every part of it operate to its maximum. The crash into the gates had made a terrible mess of the front end, but all running parts seemed to be in sync.

When he was sure that nothing would fly apart or disintegrate on the Cortina, he hit Elise again with his peripheral vision.

"I can see your head's okay . . . what about the rest of you?"

"No bones broken, but I think I may have a tough time feeding babies, if I ever have any."

Carter grinned in the dashboard lights.

She'd make it.

"Can you see all right?"

"What?"

"The road," he said. "The headlights are smashed, and one of the fog lights is pointing toward France. Can you drive with just the light from one fog light?"

She perused the road ahead for several seconds, but Carter could tell that her mind was going over far more than the onrushing asphalt or the passing countryside.

When she spoke again, the quiver was gone from her voice. In its place was a tone akin to a growling harshness.

"They . . . those two men were going to kill us, weren't they?"

"You bet your ass they were."

"I can drive in the dark."

"Good girl. We've got some lights coming up on us pretty fast. It may be that Jaguar sedan. If it is, I'm afraid we're still in the soup. It's supercharged and can outrun this toy in low."

"No more failing heart," Elise said, her lovely jaw set in a determined line. "What do you want me to do?"

"Slide over . . . under me." She wriggled her way behind and under Carter as he lifted his rear end off the seat, and then she slid her arm around until she could grasp the steering wheel.

"Got it?"

"Got it," she said.

Carter rolled away and she skillfully took over.

"Keep the accelerator on the floor. Any curves in this road can be taken full out."

She nodded, and even though her knuckles were white on the wheel she drove with skill and finesse.

When Carter was satisfied, he went to work on the Luger. He removed the bulky silencer and slid it back into its compartment on the holster. If it was the Jag behind them, silence would be superfluous. And without the silencer's long snout, Wilhelmina would be much more mobile in a close-in firefight.

Strapped to his left leg were two extra clips. One of these he jammed into Wilhelmina's butt. The other he clipped to the shoulder strap under his right armpit.

"If all my deb friends could see me now . . ."

"What?"

"Nothing," she replied, adding a low chuckle. "I was just thinking how boring my life has been up until now."

"You may wish it had stayed that way before this night is over."

Carter thought he heard her murmur "Never," but he could not be sure. He was already rolling over the seat back into the rear of the Cortina.

"He's coming fast, whoever he is."

"Is it the Jaguar?"

"Don't know . . . yet. But I will in a couple of minutes. How're we doing?"

"Right at seventy. It won't go any faster."

"Keep her there!" Carter growled.

He watched the lights come on and guessed that their speed was a good twenty miles faster than the Cortina. It had to be the boys from JOUST. No one else would be pleasure driving this road at such speeds.

"They're coming on us. When they try to pass, wait until we're almost even, then slam on your brakes."

Carter saw the back of her head nod and rolled down the rear window. They were directly behind now, about fifty yards back. They covered that in seconds and pulled out to pass.

Only the Luger's barrel and Carter's forehead were above the rim of the door.

There were three of them, two in the front and one in the rear. Bandage Face was driving.

Carter was going to take him first, but he saw the one in the rear come up with a machine pistol and changed his aim at the last second.

"Now!" Carter screamed over the roar of the engines, and he fired.

The little Cortina stood on its nose, the tires screaming and the car shuddering. They came to a full stop, and the

Jaguar sailed on by, but not before Carter got a good look at the man in its rear.

His face was gone, and his arms were hanging lifelessly out the rear window.

"Power it back up and make a fast U-turn!" Carter cried.

She did before asking what came next.

"Just the other side of that curve I saw a sign for a crossroad. Watch for it!"

At the curve she got a little too far over, and the wheels caught shoulder gravel. In seconds they were in a wild slide. A rear fender banged off a tree, but Elise held the car steady, geared down, and they were off again.

"Nice driving."

"Thanks."

Behind them, the Jag had also spun around. Just before they got around the turn, Carter could see its lights coming again.

"There's the road, or lane, or whatever it is," Carter shouted. "Turn!"

Elise was confused but had guts to spare. She cranked the wheel and slid into the turn without slackening their speed at all. If anything she pushed the Cortina harder.

The little car felt as if it were floating, then teetering, then bouncing, and suddenly they were around.

"My God, it's a dead end!" Elise cried when the car righted and their one good fog light illuminated the sign.

"I know it," Carter said, his eyes still glued to the lights behind them. "When you get to the end of this, do a one-eighty, kill your lights, and head back out."

"You mean, straight at them?"

"That's what I mean," Carter said.

Around two slight curves, they hurtled toward a grove of poplar trees. Just short of them she geared down and cranked the wheel. When she mashed the accelerator, the Cortina responded, and in seconds they were heading back.

"Go!" Carter cried when he saw the lights of the other car turn off the main road that was now in front of them.

Elise went through the gears barely using the clutch.

The Cortina bolted forward, its tail end digging into the road's soft dirt, throwing a cloud of dust up to envelop them.

In seconds they shot past the Jaguar before Bandage Face could swerve to block them.

"My God, we made it!"

"Not yet," Carter replied coolly, hefting Wilhelmina in his right hand and peering out the rear window.

Just as he had hoped, the dust from the Cortina had obscured the grove of trees at the end of the lane just long enough. The driver of the bigger car hadn't seen him soon enough and by the time he had, his momentum had carried the Jaguar broadside into the trees.

"Come around again," Carter rasped.

"What?"

"Do as I say, damnit! Do another one-eighty and then broadside into them!"

This time Elise didn't argue. She again expertly whirled the car around and drove like a demon toward the Jaguar.

"Bank right!" Carter barked, bracing his legs against the far door and steadying the Luger over his knees. "When you get aligned, let it slide and bail out!"

They slid sideways for only seconds, but to Carter it seemed like forever. At last they hit, a solid, grinding crash, and Carter came up on the seat.

Just as he had hoped, the sudden reversal to the offense by the Cortina had left the Jaguar's occupants stunned.

What Carter hadn't expected was a fourth passenger in the rear seat. He was holding his comrade's lifeless body like a shield in front of him and trying to bring a sawed-off into play.

There was only his head showing, but at this range it would be hard for anyone, let alone a marksman of Carter's ability, to miss.

Carter was looking right into the man's eyes just before they disappeared in a veil of red.

The far side door of the Jaguar opened, and the two in the front tumbled out before Carter could shift the Luger their way.

Carter reached over his head, found the door lever, and

tumbled from the car.

Elise was about ten feet away, flat on her stomach, her eyes questioning.

"Roll into the trees," Carter hissed. "Move!"

She didn't wait for a second command; she began rolling just as a revolver sounded and dust kicked up where she had been.

At the same time, Carter heard pounding feet to his right toward the rear of the cars. It was hard to fathom, but one of them was making what amounted to a suicide charge.

Instead of standing, Carter rolled around the rear of the Cortina right into the man's pumping legs. He went up and over, practically landing on Wilhelmina. Before the Luger twisted in his hands, Carter pumped two slugs into the guy's gut.

The body lifted, and Carter rolled away before it came down again.

Less than half a minute had elapsed since the initial crash. There was a drainage ditch by the end of the road. Carter dived into it and rolled.

He drew no fire, so he chanced a crawl up over the ditch's inward mound and rolled down the other side into the trees.

Still no fire.

Where was Bandage Face?

He duck-walked into the trees for about twenty yards, then angled over to a point directly away from the Jag. The fog was hardly tinting the air this far from the river, so Carter had a clear view of both cars.

He was about to spend his cover to draw fire, when he heard a rasping noise. It was close by and getting closer.

Carter relaxed, arresting all movement, even his breathing.

He squinted, focusing his eyes on the incline of the ditch in front of the Jaguar's front fender.

Blackness.

And yet he detected some form and some movement.

Bandage Face was playing commando on all fours and

heading straight for him. Evidently the guy had the same flanking idea that Carter had already executed.

Too bad.

He waited until the man was directly in front of him.

"Hey, bastard," Carter whispered, "remember Bridgit Michaels?"

The bandaged face came up as Carter squeezed and kept squeezing. When the pin clicked on empty he stopped and leaned forward.

Deftly Carter went through his pockets.

Nothing . . . except a folder containing a commercial airline ticket.

Carter stuffed it into his own pocket and stood.

"Mrs. Pearson . . . ?"

"I think you can call me Elise by now."

He saw her rise in the trees and walk toward the cars.

"Are they dead?" she asked.

"Yes."

"Good."

My, my, Carter thought, *how we can change in a very short time*.

ELEVEN

Nick Carter got through the overseas operator and waited until the hot line at Dupont Circle answered before placing the scrambler device in the mouthpiece.

In the bay of an all-night garage and service station behind him, a young mechanic was using a crowbar to pull the Jaguar's front fender away from a tire.

Since Bandage Face had conveniently used the supercharged Jag to run them to ground, Carter saw no reason not to acquire it himself to further their flight.

The garage attendant was looking his way with a heavy scowl on his face. Carter could almost read his mind: *Only a crazy American would treat such a prized piece of machinery this way!*

"Something wrong?" Carter called, placing his hand over the mouthpiece.

"Tire. Fender slashed it just enough. It's leaking . . . slow, but leaking."

"Change it!"

"Right-o."

The clicks and low hum on the overseas wire ended, bringing Carter's concentration back to the phone.

"N-3?"

"Here."

"I hope you've got something good," Hawk growled, the tenseness in his voice near the breaking point.

Carter quickly filled him in on the evening's events, including his plan to use the next few hours to pick Elise Pearson's brain.

"Good," Hawk replied. "I just hope there's a connection. Are the Brits cooperating?"

"All the way, so far. What about the *Shark*?"

"One of our AWACs thought they had a fix in the East China Sea, but they lost them. The *Shark* is loaded with the latest antidetecting devices, so it was to be expected."

"Did the fix give any clue as to direction?"

"None. She seems to be moving aimlessly, almost in a zigzag pattern."

Carter thought for a moment, closing his eyes, bringing a map of the Pacific up on his inner lids.

"But no matter how many zigs or zags, she seems to be moving north?" he said at last.

"It would seem so."

"Toward Russia."

"Maybe," Hawk said dryly.

"If that's the case . . . say Vladivostok or Nakhodka . . . what would their ETA be?"

Hawk had the information at his fingertips, letting Carter know that Washington was fearing the worst. "About eighteen hours."

"Damn," Carter muttered, and then he remembered the canceled flight ticket in his pocket. "Wait, this may mean something . . ."

He told Hawk how he had gotten the ticket and gave him a detailed physical description of Bandage Face the way he had originally looked in Bridgit Michaels's flat.

"The ticket was dated three weeks ago yesterday. He was a pro, nothing else on him, but he probably stuffed it into his inside pocket and forgot about it. It's a round-tripper, San Francisco to Tokyo, on JAL Flight 1217."

"We'll check it out from here."

"Has London sent you anything on the list of admirals?"

"Nothing yet."

Carter chewed his lip and nodded to himself. "I'll work on the woman."

"Do that. And, Nick . . ."

"Yes, sir?"

"Lean on her hard if you have to."

The connection was broken. Carter removed the

scrambler device before making his second call. It wouldn't interface with MI5's similar device, and all incoming calls to the MI5 hot number Carter was using were routinely scrambled anyway.

"Eight-eight-four-five."

Carter went through the identification process, and seconds later the now familiar voice of Sydney Jarrell came on the line.

"Where the devil are you, man? Special Branch is hotter than the hubs of hell. They want an accounting of the mission from your end!"

Carter smiled. Procedural paper work. It was the same the world over.

"Don't tell them you've heard from me yet. What did they get out of the Mainstem?"

"A great deal, it seems," Jarrell replied. "Private records indicate that a lot of skimming was taking place and has been for some time."

"It would figure," Carter said. "One hell of a lot of money would be needed to run an outfit like JOUST. Skimmed, untraceable gambling money would be a good source. What else?"

"The Mainstem was only one of a consortium of casinos—both legal and illegal—in Germany, Austria, France, as well as the U.S."

"Any idea who were the real owners?"

"Not completely . . . yet. But we've traced ownership through a ton of holding companies and come up with an outfit out of Geneva called Overcore, Ltd."

"Damn . . ."

"That's right . . . everything is secret to the Swiss. It's a dead end."

"Maybe not," Carter growled. "Get me all the specs you can . . . attorneys, bankers, etc. Maybe there's a way. I assume Special Branch caught up with the crowd at the Carstairs-Wright house?"

"We're watching."

"*What?*"

Jarrell's voice sounded red-faced. "Not much else we

can do, old boy. A man's home is his castle, you know. We can't prove there's anything going on there other than what we can see with long-range glasses."

"And what exactly is that?"

"A dinner party."

Carter's breath exhaled through his teeth. "Have your boys inquire about the busted front gate. At least that's an in."

"If you hadn't gone in and played one-man army, we might have had a chance," Jarrell retorted. "Do you have the Pearson woman?"

"Yes."

"It's probably best you bring her in."

Carter shook his head. "It might be best," he replied, "but I don't think it's safe. At least not tonight. I'm south, just off the M23 at Slough. Is there a safe house around here we can use for the rest of the night?"

"One moment."

Carter lit a cigarette and inhaled deeply as he waited.

"Do you know Bognor Regis?"

"Vaguely," Carter said. "South coast?"

"Right. Get back on the M23 to Brighton, and then west on the 27. Take a left toward the sea at the Bognor Regis turnoff. Just short of the village you'll see a sign, The Briars. Take that lane. It's a private and secluded cottage on the south cliffs there."

"Caretaker?"

"No, but the place is stocked."

"And the key is under the mat," Carter quipped.

"How did you ever guess?"

"I'll call you in the morning . . . sooner if I have anything," Carter said and hung up.

He stood for several seconds, his hand still resting on the receiver, his eyes staring.

Suddenly something odd struck him about the conversation.

How did Sydney Jarrell know the woman kidnapped from the Mainstem was Elise Pearson?

Had the Special Branch man—the little red-haired

waiter—heard Adamo call her that? Or had she been such a regular at the club that all the employees knew who she was?

Carter made a mental note to add that question to his list when he got her to the safe house and started the interrogation.

For now, he would keep his thoughts on Sydney Jarrell to himself.

"Something wrong?"

It was Elise at his shoulder. She had used the mirror in the loo well, even without comb, purse, and cosmetics.

Carter looked at her and grinned. "Nothing that three scotches and a roast beef sandwich won't fix. Let's go!"

They settled for two double orders of fish and chips to go from an all-night place in Brighton.

Carter hoped there was scotch at the safe house.

He missed The Briars turnoff the first time and went all the way into the town of Bognor Regis before turning back.

At last he found the lane and why he had missed it; the sign had been knocked down by an errant motorist.

The lane wound west, crossed 259, and went all the way to a high cliff overlooking the sea.

Carter pulled open a rickety pair of garage doors, stored the Jag, and found the front door key.

"Cozy."

"Yeah," he said. "See if you can find some booze. I'll check it all out."

The cottage was much more spacious on the inside than its exterior revealed. It had two stories, with a den, living room, dining room, and large kitchen on the first floor. The upstairs contained three bedrooms, all with private bath, and a small library.

The rear of the place was perched right on the edge of the cliff, and one side was bare rock as far as he could see. The other side was equally bare, sloping down to a plateau that also went nowhere except to the sea. The inland side was also clear for about two hundred yards.

Carter nodded to himself in appreciation of the choice.

One man with one gun and enough ammunition could hold off an army indefinitely from any one of a number of windows.

Back downstairs, Elise already had the food spread out on a small table between two chairs in front of the fireplace. And in the fireplace a small mound of peat was just popping to life.

"My God, you're domestic," Carter remarked.

"I used to watch our maids a lot," Elise said with a grin. "There's only gin."

"Figures," he said, scowling and following her gaze to a sideboard.

He found lime juice, tonic, and a very large bottle of London's best. When he had two drinks built, he slid into one of the chairs and passed a glass to Elise.

"To the warrior," she said, raising her glass.

"And the maiden," Carter replied, doing the same with his. "Let's eat!"

"You're looking very serious," she said, dabbing a napkin at the corner of her mouth.

"With my belly full, my mind has started working again. I've got a lot of questions, Elise. I think you may have some of the answers."

"Fire away," she said, slipping a cigarette from his pack.

Carter lit her cigarette, lit one for himself, and leaned back in his chair.

"Where did you meet your husband?"

"At a party in Baltimore."

"Who gave the party?"

"Oh, God, I don't know . . . it's been so long . . ."

"Remember," Carter barked, a sudden edge of steel in his voice that brought her alert.

"Well, let's see. It was . . ."

"Yes . . . ?"

"I remember! Admiral Harlan Carrington!"

Carter whipped the list from his pocket and scanned down it.

"What's that?" Elise asked, peering over the table at the paper.

"A list of English and American naval officers who were in the U.K. during the last week."

She chuckled mirthlessly. "Admiral Carrington's name wouldn't be on it, Nick. He died about a year ago."

Carter sighed. "Go on."

"With what?"

"From the beginning. Who introduced you to Ralph Pearson?"

Elise thought for a long moment and then snapped her fingers. "Lenore Grayburn."

Carter leaned forward expectantly. "What was Ralph's relationship with Lady Grayburn?"

"Friends, I guess." She shrugged. "They still are. I've been staying in her flat in London for the last month."

"Have you seen her in the meantime?"

"No . . . not until tonight, that is, at that house. We're . . . well, we're not exactly friends. She's bitchy, pushy, and I get tired of hearing her whine about how the world is going to hell."

"Why did you come to London?"

"Ralph made me. He said he was on some kind of hush-hush assignment, so I couldn't use the Maine house this summer—"

"The Maine house?"

"Yes, I have a house near Bucks Harbor. I go up there every summer."

"And did he tell you why you couldn't go this summer?"

"He just said it was needed for his assignment."

Carter felt elation, but he held it in check for the time being. "So he sent you to London."

She shrugged. "I went because it was easier than arguing. I gave up arguing with Ralph a long time ago."

Carter looked at her intently. "I take it your marriage

isn't on the best ground."

"It isn't on any ground," Elise replied, topping her words with a somewhat hysterical laugh. "It hasn't been since the end of the first year."

Without prompting, she went back to the beginning again.

After first meeting Ralph Pearson, he pursued her relentlessly. Men had pursued her before, but never like Ralph. It was a question of being swept off her feet. He was handsome, charming, and not to be dissuaded. Finally she agreed to marry him.

Everything was fine for the first year, and then, abruptly, he changed. He brooded constantly, and he never stopped talking politics. He rehashed the mistakes of the Korean and Vietnam wars. According to Ralph, the U.S. government should have used nuclear weapons immediately in those actions.

Eventually she and Pearson drifted apart. They rarely spoke, and, in the last eighteen months, rarely saw each other.

"I am planning on filing for divorce when I get back to the States."

Carter sat back and digested this before speaking again.

"Why do you think he married you in the first place?"

It hurt, and Carter could see it in her eyes. Susprisingly, after the first shock she shrugged and even managed to smile.

"To tell you the truth, I don't know. Of course, at first I thought it was because I was young and beautiful and sexy . . ."

"You are."

"Thank you, but I'm afraid that never impressed Ralph."

"Then what did?"

"Sometimes I think it was my father."

"Your father?"

"Yes. Ralph adored him . . . or at least it seemed that he did. They spent hours together during that first year of our marriage, talking physics and nuclear weaponry."

Carter jumped to his feet and began pacing, thinking out loud. "Milford Tyson was a politician. That I know, but I didn't know he had anything to do with nuclear weaponry."

"He didn't, not really," Elise replied. "I mean, he knew enough about it to do his job—"

"Job?" Carter moved back and knelt by her knees. "What job?"

Again she shrugged. "I don't know much about it . . . it was pretty secret."

"Well, tell me what you do know," Carter pressed. "This may be very important, Elise."

"Well . . ." Her forehead furrowed in concentration, and her lower lip curled between even white teeth. "Nuclear bases and missiles, as you know, are very unpopular in several countries . . ."

"Yes."

"My father made his money in construction . . . specialized architectural construction. After he retired, some Pentagon people approached him. They wanted him to build certain plants, marinas, warehouses—I don't know what all—around the world. These plants, et cetera, would ostensibly be private businesses."

"To the general population," Carter whispered. "But actually they would be missile silos, other missile launching devices, even . . . perhaps even a secret nuclear submarine base."

"I suppose so. At least, I think so."

"Which countries?"

"I don't know. That was the real secret part of it."

"Did you ever ask your father?"

"No."

"But I'll bet Ralph Pearson did."

"What do you mean?"

Carter didn't answer her.

Instead he began pacing again, smoke from his cigarette rolling behind him like a cloud as his mind clicked off the possibilities.

Milford Tyson might not tell his daughter everything,

but he might be pestered into telling his son-in-law. Especially if his son-in-law was involved in the same field.

Once Pearson had the location, and maybe even the means of access into those bases, JOUST could make their plans.

"I once mentioned JOUST to you," Carter said, suddenly whirling on her. "You reacted. Why?"

"Because it's an odd name."

"No, there has to be another reason. Think, Elise. Where did you hear it before?"

Again the nervousness. For a moment Carter thought she would clam up, but suddenly she stood and moved to the bar. She built herself a quick drink and then turned to face him.

"It was a while after Ralph and I started going our separate ways. I came home from a dinner party one night and my father was at the house. He and Ralph were in the library, and they were having an awful row."

"About JOUST?"

"I don't know, but it was mentioned several times. My father called Ralph a stupid pawn in a deadly game. He said the work he was doing was done as a deterrent, not an invitation for nuclear holocaust. He accused Ralph and his friends of setting out to destroy the world."

"Did your father mention any names?"

"I don't remember. Oh, there was an admiral . . ."

"Admiral Carrington?"

"No, I don't think so. My father thought Admiral Carrington was an idiot."

"Think, Elise . . . besides Carrington and Lady Grayburn, who else was close to Ralph? Who else was constantly in touch with him?"

After several moments of thought, she rattled off six names, both civilian and military. None of them meant anything to Carter, but he stored them away in his mental memory bank just the same.

"No one else?" he prompted.

"Lots, but I can't remember names. I'm good at faces.

Usually when I see a face from the past I can put a name to it. But names without faces? Sorry."

"It's okay. I think I might have enough to get started. Just one more thing . . ."

"Yes?"

"How often did you go to the Mainstem?"

"Oh, three, maybe four times since I've been here."

"Why?"

"What?"

"I mean, why the Mainstem? There must be thirty, forty clubs like it in London, and most of them more popular than the Mainstem."

"Simple." Elise shrugged. "Ralph has a member's card there. I just used it."

The pounding in Carter's head suddenly ceased. Snapping his fingers and wringing his hands, he began a systematic search for the phone.

It was a whole new tack.

Instead of trying to dig out names of directors' boards and corporate bigwigs who might have their fingers in the ownership of the casino, what about the actual lists of *members*?

Those lists would be held very confidential and would appear completely innocent.

Carter would also lay odds that mercenaries working for JOUST collected their pay, and probably their espense money, through the clubs. What better way to disburse money—especially blood money—than through gambling casinos?

Nothing on the books, not a trace.

He found the phone on the back bar and began to dial. Halfway through the sequence he heard the unmistakable click.

There was a bug on the line.

He slammed the receiver down on the cradle and went over the choices.

It was an MI5 safe house that was probably used by several other services at one time or another.

Why shouldn't there be a bug on the phone? It was only natural and probably just a recording machine that was monitored once a week.

But it still bothered Carter.

He thought again of Sydney Jarrell. What if he was another link in MI5 to JOUST? Carter would be spilling his guts to the very person who could keep the information quiet.

But if it was Jarrell, he also knew Carter and Elise's location.

Carter checked his watch. It was three in the morning. Outside, it was pitch black and the fog was rolling in.

The cottage was practically a fortress.

He decided not only *not* to make the call, but to wait three hours or so until dawn to make a move.

If there were JOUST people out there somewhere, or if they were watching the main arteries into London, he and Elise would be much safer right where they were.

"You're thinking again."

She had crept up behind him as silently as a cat and now stood at his shoulder.

"Yeah. I've decided we stay put until dawn after all."

"Good. Are you through with the questions for a while?"

"Yes," he smiled, "until I've digested what you've already told me."

"Terrific. Can I take a bath then? I think I smell like a horse."

"Sure. There are two master suites upstairs. Take your pick. I'm going to sit down here for the night."

She freshened her drink one more time, and he watched her glide up the stairs.

It was quite a sight.

Just below the black turtleneck, Lenore Grayburn's slacks fit Elise Pearson like a second skin.

When she had disappeared, Carter made the rounds. He slid the safety bolts and draped the chains on all three doors—front, side, and rear.

Every window downstairs had iron grillwork on the

outside plus safety locks on the windows themselves.

If anyone tried to get in, it would take a blowtorch and a well-placed brick. By that time he would have awakened the dead, Nick Carter, and Wilhelmina.

Upstairs he checked the bedroom and small library, and found the same fortification. The master suite he would use had French doors leading out onto a balcony, but it would take Spider Man to reach it.

It was a sheer brick and rock drop several hundred feet to the sea and rocks below.

He tapped on Elise's partially open door and got no answer.

When he popped his head inside, he heard why. The door to the bathroom was open, and he could hear the sound of splashing water beyond it.

He checked and secured the windows on both sides of this room, then opened the French doors and stepped out onto the balcony.

He could barely see the drive below through the fog, but the brick front of the house was free of vines or anything else that could be used for scaling purposes.

He locked the French doors behind him and started across the room just as Elise stepped from the bath.

"Oh . . . I didn't hear . . ."

For the second time that night Carter saw a naked Elise Pearson.

But, for some reason, this time he was jolted by the sight.

Her perfect breasts jutted forward, and they seemed to have an odd glow all their own in the room's harsh light. Her womanly hips and rounded thighs seemed to caress the space between them.

A towel was wrapped turban-style around her wet hair. On seeing Carter, she whipped it off and held it in front of her.

"You didn't do that earlier," he murmured.

"I . . . I didn't have a towel then."

"True."

They were about ten feet apart, and suddenly she started

edging toward him. Carter didn't move. In seconds of silence she stopped three feet from him.

There was still dampness on her face from the bath, and Carter thought he detected a troubled brightness in her eyes.

She stepped closer until her warm breath bathed his face. The sweet scent of her freshly scrubbed body filled his nostrils.

"Somehow . . . being naked in front of you before was different. This is . . . so . . ."

"What?"

Suddenly, with a savage cry, Elise threw herself against him, her still damp breasts pillowing across his chest.

"You'd better believe it's different now," Carter growled, sweeping her into his arms.

The following hour was one of passion and pain, an hour that Nick Carter would not forget for a long time.

On the bed, with her lips pressed almost cruelly to his, Elise tore at his clothes with feverish haste.

When he was naked at last, she thrust toward him eagerly, molding her body to his.

Another kiss, her tongue invading his lips like a hot iron of flesh to find his. Her strong hands explored his back, sweeping his body, urging him to press even harder against her.

She was a volcano of sheer desire, but there was feminine tenderness at her core. It was as if the tumult and frustrations of the last four years could be wiped away with a single lingering moment of love.

And then Carter felt the tide of desire and passion brim over in his own body.

He curled his powerful arms around her in an insistent yet tender embrace and slipped one leg between her quivering thighs.

They moved together, drowning their senses in the taste, the touch, and the smell of one another.

"Don't . . . don't tease me," she gasped. "Hurry!"

Liquid warmth spread throughout Carter's body as they joined. Every moan he made was matched by her in perfect harmony.

Again he kissed her and felt her body arch beneath him.

But Carter held off, wanting to savor all of her body and, at the same time, bring her the satisfaction she so urgently sought.

"Nick!" she cried breathlessly, ripping her fingers along his back to urge him on.

Carter increased his tempo, the depth of his thrusts. He was a man who knew how to draw sensual ecstasy from a woman's body, and he was doing it now with Elise Pearson.

Another startled cry erupted from her parted lips, and her body came up to his in an aching, jolting caress.

"Nick . . ."

"Yes, yes, now," he eagerly whispered in her ear.

Passion spilled from both their bodies at once, and then Carter fell across her, weary, satiated, but fulfilled.

They lay silent for several moments until the whirling room came back into focus.

"It's been a while," she whispered.

"I could tell."

"It was wonderful . . ."

"For both of us," he said and cradled her head closer to his.

It was the combination of the breaking dawn and the sound of a car somewhere in the distance that awakened Carter.

He checked his watch. It was 6:30.

He looked over at the sleeping form in the bed next to him. Some time during the hours of sleep Elise had covered them both and then crawled back in beside him.

The car's engine was growing louder.

Carter slid from the bed and found his clothes. By the time he was dressed she was partially awake, sitting up in bed, rubbing her eyes.

"What is it?" she said and yawned.

"I don't know yet. There's a car outside. It sounds like it's coming up our lane."

Suddenly all vestiges of sleep were gone, and she was bolting from the bed. "What are we going to do?"

"*I'm* going to find out who it is. You get dressed."

Carter took the stairs three at a time, checking the loads in Wilhelmina as he ran.

He parted the curtains over the narrow, slotted windows at the side of the door and peered out.

It was a big, black Daimler, with heavily frosted glass at the windows. It rounded the last turn near the trees and then turned through the twin pillars of concrete at the head of the lane.

Carter scooted to one of the front windows, unlocked it, and slid it up six inches, just enough for a firing slot.

The Daimler rocked to a halt directly in front of the door. Both front doors opened and three big college types in dark suits piled out.

Carter spotted artillery under the jackets of all three.

Two of them opened the rear doors. Carter brought the Luger's barrel up to the window when he saw Sydney Jarrell climb from his side of the car.

He was about to call out to the man to stop right there, when the other occupant of the rear seat stepped around the tail end of the Daimler.

It was Owen Hamilton.

Carter breathed an audible sigh of relief and moved back to the front door. In seconds he had the chain down, the bolts off, and the door opened.

"You're a sight for sore eyes," Carter said, stepping out onto the front stoop.

"I would rather imagine," Hamilton replied, moving around Jarrell and walking toward the door. "You've had yourself quite a night."

"I was planning on coming back up to London this morning."

"I thought as much and decided it would be better if we had a briefing down here first."

Carter stepped aside, allowing the commander to move by him into the cottage.

"Would you mind very much putting that away?" Hamilton intoned, nodding toward the Luger still in Carter's hand at his side.

Carter leathered Wilhelmina and moved to the center of the room where Hamilton stood.

"Sorry. After last night I really don't know what to expect."

Carter heard Jarrell and the others file in behind him and the door close. Out of the corner of his eye he saw part of Elise's shoulder and some of her blond hair around the corner of the stairs.

"You can come down, Elise."

Carter could almost hear her sigh of relief as she walked down the last section of stairs and entered the room.

She was only a few feet from them when Owen Hamilton turned to greet her.

"Hello, my dear."

"Admiral Hamilton."

"Admiral?" Carter said.

"Yes, my boy. It's often the case in the military on our side of the pond."

"What is?" Carter asked, straining to keep his hands at his sides.

"When an officer retires from active service and then enters the civil service, he takes the rank of commander."

"And you retired as . . . ?"

"As a vice-admiral."

Carter was already rolling to the side, clawing under his left armpit for Wilhelmina, when a powerful blow caught him at the back of the neck.

A second hit just behind his ear brought on total blackness.

The last thing he heard was Elise Pearson's voice . . . screaming.

TWELVE

Carter swam awake with a blinding pain just behind his eyes and a dull throb at the back of his head.

He experimented with consciousness by blinking one eye, then the other, then both.

Eventually the pain subsided enough so that he was able to leave his eyes open and case his surroundings.

He was lying on a thin-mattressed iron cot. A small round table was in the center of the room, and beside it stood a worse-for-wear wicker chair.

Sunlight slanted in yellow bars from a dirty-paned single window high up in the brick wall. All the walls were brick, and there was one heavy, oak door with a peek-slot in its center.

And then he took a look at himself. He had been stripped to the waist, and his shoes had been removed. Even his AXE-designed watch with the three-foot length of piano wire coiled around its works had been removed from his wrist.

Carter slid his right hand down to his crotch . . . and smiled.

They had searched him but had not stripped him completely. Chances are they had merely patted him down from waist to ankles.

Pierre, his tiny bomb with the deadly fumes, was still in place alongside the rest of the Carter family jewels.

On shaky legs Carter made it across the room where he thought he had spotted a rusty water faucet protruding from the bricks.

It was, and it was working.

He flipped it on and stuck his head under the faucet. The cold water burned the gash behind his right ear, but it eventually drove the cobwebs from his brain.

After a few slow, very slow, exercises to get his body working, he slid the table over to the wall beneath the window.

Even through the filthy pane the sunlight outside was blinding until his eyes adjusted.

It looked like some kind of small military encampment. He counted another twenty low, squat brick structures much like the one he was in. They were arranged in an unconnected circle, and beyond them was a fifteen-foot fence with another two feet of barbed wire at the top.

He could see two occupied guard towers just beyond the fence to his right and left. The men in them wore regulation British Special Forces fatigues and carried Sten guns at the ready across their chests.

The expressions on their faces made Carter wonder if World War III had already begun.

He was about to climb down, when a man appeared from between the buildings to his right.

The man was young and not too big, but solidly built, with neatly trimmed blond hair. Unlike the men in the towers, this one wore cord slacks and a matching jacket over a yellow knit shirt. Instead of a Sten, Carter could see the bulge of a heavy hand piece under his jacket on the left side.

Trailing directly at his heels was a brace of big, black Dobermans. The muscular animals made no sound, but their silent, narrow, dangerous snouts seemed alert to every smell and sound around them.

The dogs trailed the man all the way across the compound. Just before reaching a building on the other side, a door burst open and Sydney Jarrell—or what was left of him—was thrust through its opening.

Like Carter, Jarrell was peeled to the waist and shoeless. Unlike Carter's single gash behind the ear, Jarrell was a mess. His face was pulpy and bleeding in several places. Even from such a distance Carter could see that one eye was swollen shut and the man's nose was broken.

If that wasn't enough, both hands were heavily bandaged. The bandages looked fresh, but already they were turning crimson.

Well, Carter thought, *so much for Jarrell being part of JOUST*. Maybe.

Two men, also in casual civilian dress, emerged from the doorway behind Jarrell. They exchanged a few words with the Dobermans' keeper and went back inside, closing the door behind them.

The man in the yellow shirt said something to Jarrell and gave him a slight push. Jarrell whirled but came up short when the Dobermans growled and tensed in preparation to spring.

Jarrell spat an oath at them and the man through his bloody, swollen lips, and shrugged. He turned and headed directly toward Carter.

From somewhere Carter heard a door open. It was quickly followed by more growls from the Dobermans, and then the door in the next room was unlocked and opened.

Carter jumped from the table and pressed his ear to the wall. He could hear both men's voices, but they were too muffled to distinguish words.

He heard the door open and close again, and then a key turned in the lock.

So Jarrell was in the cell-like room next to his, Carter thought. Where was Elise?

He started to drag the table back to the center of the room, when he heard a rattling sound in the wall between him and Jarrell. When it came again, Carter looked down and saw the water faucet moving.

Quickly he dropped to his knees and put his eye to the crack around the faucet.

About a foot away he saw another eye.

"Jarrell?" he whispered.

"Yes. How's your head, old man?"

"Sore," Carter replied with a grunt, "but not like yours. How bad is it?"

"My face, a few ribs. I'll live."

"What about your hands?"

There was a brief pause before Jarrell spoke again. "They severed the end joint on two of my fingers."

"Jesus," Carter hissed. "What the hell for?"

"Hamilton must have thought I was on to him. I wasn't, but he's not taking any chances. They wanted to know what you told Washington last night before you spoke with me, when I gave you the location of the safe house. Of course I didn't tell them anything because you told me nothing. But they wanted to be sure."

"So they cut your fingers off?"

There was a low chuckle from the other side of the wall. "They are a bit daft, I do believe . . . totally immersed in this cause of theirs. No one is going to stand in their way. I've an idea you're in for the same treatment as soon as they figure you're bright-eyed again."

"What's it all about?" Carter asked, sold now that Jarrell was on his side.

"Don't know it all, old chap, but I must have put too much together for Hamilton's liking."

"How so?"

"Last night, about an hour after your call . . ."

"Yeah?"

"Got a hot line call from a chap named Hawk . . . one of your people."

"I know him," Carter said dryly, not bothering to inform Jarrell that few people knew about AXE, and even fewer knew David Hawk.

"They traced the user of that Japan Air Lines ticket you have."

"And . . . ?"

"His name is Bernard Kettering. He is—"

"*Was*. He's dead," Carter said, surprised that no one had stumbled across the Cortina and the bodies since he and Elise had abandoned them.

"Be that as it may, Kettering was a colonel in your

Special Forces. Left the service in a bit of a huff evidently after Vietnam and soon after became a hired gun for several ultra-right-wing causes. About two years ago he was jailed in Africa for an assassination attempt on a socialist presidential candidate. He was sentenced to hang, but a few days before the execution a highly trained military team broke him out of prison."

"JOUST . . ." Carter murmured.

"It would appear so . . . now."

"What's the connection with Japan?"

"That's just it. Your Mr. Hawk told me to relay to you that they traced him to Noshiro, in northern Japan. Then, for five days, he dropped out of sight, only to show up again in Noshiro."

"Doesn't sound like much," Carter growled.

"That's what I thought, but I was a Royal Air Force navigator before I got into the copper business . . ."

"And . . . ?"

"And Mr. Hawk also said they got another partial fix on the *Shark*. I drew some coordinates between the first and second fix—Noshiro, Japan, and Vladivostok."

A bell rang in the back of Carter's mind. "And you came up with Longitude 140, Latitude 40!"

"That I did . . . south of Noshiro, about halfway to Oga Pen. According to topography maps, that's a pretty desolate area."

"But a few years ago the U.S. government built something there," Carter said, thinking of Milford Tyson.

"Not the government, exactly, but a private English-American conglomerate called Cal-Brit Ltd. It's a far-reaching company. They built a cannery in Japan, a huge fishing boat anchorage in Scotland, an underground steel smelter in West Germany . . ."

Jarrell rattled on, but Carter's mind was already racing ahead.

It was all pretty clear now, and all pretty involved. Milford Tyson had been employed by Cal-Brit, a large conglomerate that appeared to be privately owned but was, in fact, a joint U.K.-U.S.-owned front.

A very secret front, kept that way so that the left hand wouldn't know what the right hand was doing.

Well, now it had boomeranged.

Tyson's job was to build these places, and within them were storage areas of different kinds for nuclear deterrent. Even when built, they wouldn't be manned . . . not until the antinuclear factions of the host countries became so strong that our missiles would be forced underground, into hiding.

Any one of these bases would be ready-made for JOUST.

Once Pearson—through Elise—got close to Old Man Tyson and breached security, JOUST could formulate strike plans.

Ten-to-one, Kettering's job had been to lead a strike force to take control of the Japanese fishery near Noshiro.

That's where the U.S.S. *Shark* was probably moored at that very moment, lying in wait with four deadly missiles directly across the Sea of Japan from Vladivostok, Russia.

Jarrell's voice came back into Carter's awareness.

" . . . so I really didn't know if I had anything or not, but when Commander Hamilton arrived at Headquarters, I gave it to him, just in case."

"And also told him where Elise and I were stashed."

"Yes. He suggested we all drive down and escort you back to London as a security matter."

"So you never guessed Hamilton, either."

"Good Lord, no," Jarrell replied. "I was going through the lists of active admirals. I never thought of *retired* admirals. I'm afraid . . ."

"What is it?" Carter asked, catching a new tone in the other man's voice.

Jarrell heaved a deep sigh. "It was Hamilton who supervised my 'interrogation' just now. He . . . he was a different man. In fact, I do believe he is insane."

"And those around him are equally as radical?"

"Oh, quite. They firmly believe—even Lady Grayburn—that if we don't strike first, and *now,* the

Soviet Union will do it first . . . and soon. Commander Hamilton called it 'a war to avert a war.' "

"Where are we now?" Carter asked.

"In Lancashire, near the Irish Sea. It's an old prisoner-of-war camp turned over to Special Branch years ago for training purposes."

"Know anything about the layout?"

"A bit," Jarrell replied, "I was trained here myself. One moment . . ."

Carter heard soft movement from beyond the wall, and then Jarrell was back.

"It's our lady friend. She's in the room on my other side. We have the same means of communication. Wants to know how your head is."

Carter felt a pang of guilt jab into his brain. In all the time he had been talking to Jarrell, he hadn't once thought about Elise.

"Tell her I'm fine. How is she?"

"Fine . . . banged up a bit, but they considered her a noncombatant, so they were fairly gentlemanly. That's the quirk of all this, Carter. Each of them considers himself an officer and a gentleman. They can't understand why we're trying to stop them, when what they're doing is only for the good of Queen and Country."

"I'm not so sure the Queen or much of the country would agree with them."

Jarrell answered something, but Carter was already headed for the table, dragging it back to the window. He had heard a car drive into the compound.

It was the black Daimler, surrounded by the same college types who had accompanied Hamilton to the safe house.

Only now they were all in full, bemedaled uniform, Vice-Admiral Owen Hamilton included.

He stood at the Daimler's rear door, poised to slide into the seat and speaking with Lenore Grayburn. She was nodding in agreement to everything he said, and now and then flicking her glance toward the building where Carter,

Jarrell, and Elise Pearson were being held.

At last Hamilton and his "staff" got into the car. Carter could swear that Lenore Grayburn was almost at attention as the big car pulled away.

It was barely out of sight beyond the compound when she turned to the young man with the Dobermans.

She spoke.

He nodded.

And Carter knew it was his turn.

He could almost see the man's small, chill, expressionless eyes fall on the window where Carter stood as he and the dogs moved toward the building.

THIRTEEN

The narrow-eyed young man did little guarding or herding. The dogs did it all.

They went across the clearing in the center of the compound, with Nick Carter in the lead and the man bringing up the rear while the dogs trotted, one on each side of Carter.

Just beyond the row of buildings—but still inside the fence—was a huge mound of grassed-over earth. Sprouting from the top of the mound was a large disc and several smaller antennae.

A long ramp led down into the side of the mound, and at the bottom was a uniformed guard and a door. The guard opened the door for Carter and his entourage with a "Good day to ya, sir!"

"Maybe for you," Carter growled.

A small anteroom led into a large tunnel. On both sides of a wide aisle there was a beehive of communications activity. Men and women—all in the uniforms of their various countries—sat manning radio and computer equipment.

If Carter had held any doubts about the size of JOUST, they were gone now.

"Quite a layout," he said, meaning it.

"It was an old bomb shelter," the man behind him replied. "We converted it when we requisitioned the base."

"How do all these people cover their absences from their real duty?"

"This *is* their real duty," came the harsh reply. "Right through that door at the end of the aisle."

Carter moved.

Beyond the door was a long, fluorescent-lighted hallway with closed doors every few feet on both sides.

"Last one on your right."

It was an office, sterile but well appointed, with a large oak desk, several pieces of leather furniture, a wet bar, and one wall lined with more communications equipment.

"Have a seat, sir, she'll be with you in a minute." The guard moved to the door and pointed at the two Dobermans. "Sit. Stay!"

They flopped to their haunches, and the guard left. Carter eased himself into one of the two chairs facing the desk and then spotted what looked like a cigarette box on the desk top.

He started to rise, but quickly sat back down when both of the big dogs rose with him, low, ominous growls rolling from their long throats.

"Just testing you," Carter said brightly, very carefully crossing his legs and leaning back in the chair.

Ten minutes later a door-panel built into the wall behind the desk opened, and Lady Lenore Grayburn herself glided like a tall, raven-haired feline into the room.

Carter made a move to stand, and the dogs growled.

"Hush!" she said.

They immediately went back to their haunches as the woman moved around the desk with her hand extended.

"I'm so happy to meet you at last, Mr. Carter!"

Carter ignored the hand.

"Are those cigarettes in that box?"

She quickly recovered without registering the snub and snatched the box from the desk. "Yes, help yourself. A drink?"

"Is it poisoned?"

Her full red lips pressed into a hard line. "Please don't be childish, Mr. Carter. We're both civilized and, in a way, trying to achieve the same ends. We merely use different means."

"Lady Grayburn, if you'll pardon the expression, I

think you're full of shit. Yes, I'll have that drink . . . brandy, if you have it."

A slight tic developed in her right cheek and eye, but other than that she gave no indication that she had even heard him.

As he lit the cigarette and welcomed the harsh, nonfiltered smoke deep into his lungs, Carter cased her.

Long, almost manly, but still very graceful strides took her across the room to the bar. Every movement was economical as she poured two snifters of brandy and returned.

She wore a very expensively tailored tweed skirt and matching jacket. Beneath it was one of those satiny blouses that marvelously enhance a woman's breasts while reminding the viewer that the blouse's wearer is conservatively dressed.

Her hair was parted in the center and fit sleek against her scalp like a glossy black helmet. She had blue-black eyes, deep set above high cheekbones, a long, haughty nose, and the kind of thin lips and jutting chin that denotes a will of steel beneath the surface.

On this, his second closeup of her, Carter got the same impression of Lenore Grayburn's eyes: they were cold and emotionless, with a vacuum behind them.

Carter accepted the glass, swirled, sniffed, and drank.

"Our doctors examined you while you were still unconscious. There is no concussion, and the cut required only four stitches."

"I don't know how to thank you," Carter said icily. "It's a pity you aren't as concerned with Sydney Jarrell's welfare."

"Oh, but we are," she replied with equally icy calm. "We just knew that he could be persuaded to tell us everything. With the *right* persuasion, he would tell us the truth."

"So when you cut his fingers off and his story didn't change, you knew he was telling the truth."

"Precisely," she said, lifting the glass to her lips.

Carter had seen cool ones, but Lenore Grayburn very nearly topped the pack. Her calmness, combined with the lack of any depth in her stony eyes, sent quivers up his spine that he rarely felt.

"And do you plan on playing the same little games with me?"

"Of course not, Mr. Carter. You're an entirely different breed than Mr. Jarrell. Such excessive use of torture would only prevent you from telling us anything."

"Good," Carter said, "then we understand one another."

"I hope we will . . . by the time this conversation is over. Another?"

"No, thanks, it's the middle of the day. I may have work to do yet this afternoon."

The implication of his words wasn't lost on her. She smiled, but once again Carter noticed that there was no meaning, no warmth nor humor, in the smile or the face behind it.

The woman was made of ice.

For the next half hour Nick Carter sat smoking in stony silence as Lenore Grayburn espoused the credo of JOUST.

In almost every facet, it was about the way he had figured.

The newest wrinkle, of course, was the knowledge that the brains and driving force behind the operation was Owen Hamilton.

As a young man, forty years before, Hamilton had spent a great deal of time in emerging Nazi Germany. He had literally been on the scene during Hitler's rise to power.

It was then he had been imbued with the almost fanatical belief that the one terror civilized man could not condone was Communism.

At this point Carter had to agree with Hamilton.

For years, while Hamilton was doing intelligence work

around the world, he had warned anyone who would listen of the Red Menace; usually no one listened.

Ten years earlier, in the early seventies, with liberalism at its peak, Hamilton decided to do something about his beliefs.

JOUST was already a reality but made up of tired, many retired, wealthy American and English capitalists. These men talked, but they did little in the way of action.

Hamilton and a few other silent and secret members of JOUST decided that action was necessary. Most of these men were of the military persuasion. They concluded that the only solution to the Communist problem was military might: first strike.

With money from the older JOUST members, and Hamilton's genius for organization, JOUST became active.

"And where along the line," Carter asked, "did you come in?"

"Contrary to what you may have heard or read, my father was not the idle 'lord of the manor' he was painted in the press."

"Then what exactly was he?"

"Of those 'older' members of JOUST," Lenore replied, the pride evident in her voice, "my father was always for the solution we are now pursuing."

"And you?"

"I, Mr. Carter, am my father's daughter."

"So you follow Hamilton."

"Owen is a genius," she replied, her eyes sparkling perhaps a bit too brightly.

"He's a despot," Carter offered, "who will kill half the world."

Her spine stiffened visibly. "We have done studies on first strike," she countered. "With the organization we have at hand, the kill ratio will be much smaller than you might suppose."

The faint chill that had been tickling Carter's back now turned to a wide stripe of ice.

Idly he wondered if a farmer and his family of five in the Ukraine or a garage mechanic and his new bride in Kansas would agree with her statistics.

He got off the subject and picked her brains to see if what Jarrell had come up with—and his own conclusions—were correct.

They were, almost to the letter.

Milford Tyson had been the key they had been looking for. The Japanese fishery/cannery-cum-missile base and underground nuclear submarine berth were perfect.

"So you'll start it all with missiles from the U.S.S. *Shark*?"

She nodded. "But that will be quickly followed by two more missiles fired directly from this base, and two more from West Germany. The communications—both here and at command headquarters in Maine . . ."

"Elise Pearson's summer home?"

"It has been converted."

"I figured as much," Carter sighed, mashing out the cigarette and lighting another.

"From here and Maine we are linked to a satellite, which in turn inferfaces us with NATO, Washington, and London."

"So when your big boom goes off in Vladivostok, you precede it by a few seconds to the Western alliance."

"Exactly," she smirked. "It's not hard to understand. The Western powers will see the futility of not going along with the strike, and they will launch as well."

She paused, lighting a cigarette herself and blowing two thin, very precise streams of smoke from her thin, very precise nostrils.

"When it's all over, we will be hailed as heroes and all of us will be back on the same side."

"If any of us are left alive," Carter said dryly.

"We have taken that into account, Mr. Carter. Each of our requisitioned bases have bomb shelters such as this. Near the Maine headquarters, a hillside has been gutted and converted into a bomb shelter. From there Admiral

Hamilton will be able to aid in directing first strike even if Washington is destroyed."

It was then that the whole became all too clear to Carter.

Owen Hamilton had watched Adolf Hitler's rise. Just how much had he admired the man's method and ideology?

Could it be that Hamilton was replacing Brown Shirts with JOUST members, and V-2s and blitzkrieg with the ultimate, quick solution . . . nuclear holocaust?

And then, out of the chaos, he would step forward as the only true savior of democracy, on his terms.

If that wasn't it, on the button, Carter was pretty sure it was close.

"Which brings us to you," Lenore Grayburn said, moving closer until she stood directly above Carter.

"Me?"

"You are quite an extraordinary man, Mr. Carter."

"So was Harry Lords."

"No. Harry was a fool. All the while he thought he was seducing me, I was in reality seducing him. I truly wanted to win him over to our cause as much as I wanted to find out how much other penetration agencies such as yours had made into our organization."

"And when you found out very little, you put him in front of a firing squad."

"But not without a choice. He chose that instead of joining us. Very foolish." A slight smile curved her full lips. "I don't think . . . Nick . . . that you are as foolish. As I said before, you are an extraordinary man, a man of action. Owen admires you."

"Even after I wiped out his best at Grayburn House?"

"Even more so after that. A man like you could be invaluable to us during reconstruction."

"Yes," Carter nodded, "I suppose I could . . . as an enforcer."

"It would be no different than your job right now, and you would be fighting for the same things."

She dropped to her haunches in such a way that her

breasts raked Carter's arm on the way down.

Not surprisingly, nothing stirred in him.

"Like Owen, Nick, *I* admire you. You are the kind of man who doesn't waste time with words. You let your actions speak for you. You are the breed of man who will be needed when the time comes."

Carter found it difficult as hell to return her direct stare. Her eyes were like those of a serpent; they stared but said nothing.

"That I would have to think about."

"I'll consider that enough of an answer . . . for now."

She stood, this time without the breast brushing, and walked around the desk. She pushed a button on a console of buttons and then spoke again.

"You have forty-eight hours to make a decision. Beyond that, your decision will mean little either way, and I will be much too busy to worry about it one way or the other."

"How's chances of a little talk with Hamilton?"

She shook her head. "Impossible. He's already on his way to the United States."

"Maine?"

"Yes. Now, about the other matter. How much did you relay to your superiors last night, before you spoke to Jarrell and took the woman to the safe house?"

Carter thought for a moment. Because of the tap on the safe house phone, they knew he had not talked to Washington after interrogating Elise. Because of what he had told Jarrell earlier, they knew he had not put together the pieces about her father and her husband.

He decided that the truth—as a hedge against time—was the best bet.

"Nothing. And that's the truth."

Her stare bored into and through him for several seconds before she smiled her vacant smile and nodded.

"I believe you."

The door opened and the dog keeper glided into the room.

"Take him back and have the doctors check his wound again. Also have a good meal prepared. Steak and kidney pie, Mr. Carter?"

"That would be delicious, Lady Grayburn."

This time across the compound, Carter cased it all. He located the motor pool, the armory, and even the cement rises that probably held the two missiles Lenore Grayburn had mentioned.

It was all secure. Mostly.

But Carter was pretty sure that if he could get out of his cell, he could raise a lot of hell.

The question was . . . would it do any good?

FOURTEEN

After devouring the promised meal and holding still for the doctor's probing fingers and a fresh bandage, Carter went to work.

Through the crack in the wall at the water pipe he instructed Jarrell and, in turn, Elise to watch the shift changes in the tunnel and the tower guards. Also, he wanted as close a count as possible of the free-roaming guards in the compound, and how many guards went in and out of the guard room in the building where the three of them were housed.

"Are we trying a break, old boy?"

"We are," Carter whispered, "if I can find me a key to get out of here first."

That done, he started examining his room inch by inch.

He went over the walls brick by brick and wasn't surprised to find that craftsmen had put the building together. They were painstakingly fitted. So much so that only sharp tools would serve to dislodge them.

Two hours later he had finished with the side and exterior walls.

Nothing.

Now he moved to the inside wall containing the door. It was solid oak, and the framing was equally as strong. Even the hinges were on the outside.

Carter stepped back and studied the door. For what, he didn't know. Even if he could get through it, there was a long, bare hall on the other side with another brick wall at one end of it and the guard's room at the other.

But the door was the only way.

Tools . . . *a* tool.

Lightly his fingers slid over his belt and then the buckle. The tongue of the belt buckle, as small as it was, could be used as a tool.

Quickly he slid the belt off and wrapped the leather around his hand.

He started on the nails around the framing. There were at least two dozen of them on one side alone. God only knew how long it would take him or how many nails would have to be removed before the framing would be loose enough to jiggle, but it was the only avenue of escape he could figure out.

It was more tedious than difficult. The tongue of the buckle kept bending, and several times he had to run it over the bricks to get a sharper edge on it. This done, he would attack the nail again, only to blunt it again.

Sweat poured into his eyes, and his fingers ached from the pressure of holding the buckle just right.

Then, slowly, the nailhead began to give. When it was out far enough, he went to work on it with his fingers.

"C'mon, damn you . . . come out!"

It did, and Carter went to work on the next one.

The minutes dragged by, and the light from the window faded.

Outside it was becoming night. Inside Carter continued to work, his eyes straining at the nails in the dim light from the one small overhead bulb.

It was about an hour after full darkness when he heard footsteps and voices in the hall outside.

They opened Elise's door first, then Jarrell's. Carter could hear the clatter of metal on metal and knew that it would be their supper.

He counted the nails on the tile floor at his feet: ten.

Would the door facing hold when they opened it?

He had no time to even partially reinsert the nails.

A key was already turning in the lock.

Carter scooped the nails into his hands and dived for the cot. He lay on his back and placed his hands behind his head. Carefully he arranged the nails in his fists so that the points protruded a half inch from the heels of his hands.

If the loose doorframe was spotted, they would be his only weapons.

It was the dog keeper, complete with his charming pets.

The Dobermans stayed in the doorway while he crossed to the table and set down the dinner tray.

"Lady Grayburn would like to know if you've come to any decision yet."

"And if I have?"

"I'm to relay it to her."

For the briefest of moments Carter thought his vigil at the nails might not be needed. If he could deliver his answer in the Lady's boudoir—without the dogs—he might get the run of the compound after dispensing with her.

But by sending word through this lackey, that was out of the question.

"Tell her I'm still thinking it over."

The man shrugged and returned to the door. Carter held his breath and squeezed the nails tighter in his fists as he saw him lean against the jamb.

It moved, barely, but it moved.

"My brother was the one in the van."

"What?" Carter asked.

"The man you wasted in the van outside Bridgit Michaels's flat. He was my brother."

Carter shrugged. "Fortunes of war."

"Yeah . . . 'tis. I hope you decide not to take the lady's offer."

The implication was only too clear. If Carter said "No," he was meat for this lad and his dogs. Hamilton and Lady Grayburn didn't plan on keeping prisoners around who didn't agree with their philosophy.

" 'Til morning . . . bloke."

"Ta-ta," Carter said, watching with all his concentration as the door settled back into place.

It fit, but there was a tiny gap of light that hadn't been there before.

A quick check of the tray for silverware. The tongue on

the belt buckle was wearing down.

A paper carton of milk, two bowls, and the tray itself.

No silverware.

The edge of a bowl or the tray could be used, but scraping them down to size on the bricks would surely be loud enough to whet a guard's curiosity.

He went back to work with the buckle.

Four nails later, Jarrell's voice reached him through the wall. Carter scurried to the water faucet.

"Yeah?"

"Don't know if we've got it down to the man, but I think we've got a count."

"How many?" Carter asked.

"The shift changed in the tunnel. They must do most everything in the daytime. Twenty-three went out, three went in."

"And the guards?"

"Two in the towers and two walking the compound. As near as we can figure, our guardroom in this building is it for their breaks. There are six more in there, probably doing two hours on and four off with the four outside."

"Good enough. Have you got any reading on the time?"

"Figuring from sundown, I'd say it's somewhere between nine and ten o'clock."

Carter did a quick calculation. At this rate he was up to three nails an hour.

One o'clock in the morning would be just about right.

In quick, to-the-point sentences, Carter explained what he was doing.

"Good luck, old boy."

Carter went back to the nails.

The hardest part was done. The more the jamb could be worked, the easier it was to remove the nails.

At last, with only two nails holding the board at the top, he pried it off. From there on it was a piece of cake.

Using the pried-away board as a lever, he jammed the inner frame until the bar of the lock was free. Then a gentle push and the door swayed open.

The hall was dimly lit, with only three bare bulbs along its ceiling.

Outside his cell, Carter again pried the frame and swung the door back into place. He then placed the board as flat as he could on the floor against the wall and moved down the hallway.

The door to the guardroom was open.

There were five of them: two asleep on cots, two playing cards at a small table, and another brewing fresh coffee over a hot plate.

Carter unzipped his pants, reached under his shorts to his crotch, and worked at the skinlike adhesive with his thumbnail. In seconds it gave, and Pierre dropped into his palm.

Pierre was about the size of a large marble, with what looked like a hairline crack running all the way around it. The crack was actually a break in the gas bomb's outer skin. Through it came the instantly deadly fumes that could not be seen or smelled.

Carter twisted each side of the crack until he heard the faint click. When it came, he rolled the bomb into the room and started to count.

"What the hell was that?"

"I dunno."

"It went under Paul's cot . . ."

"Watch it! It might be a rat!"

"Five . . ." Carter whispered and slammed himself against the door.

A couple of them banged against it from the other side, but rather feebly, with no force.

Pierre was already going to work.

The little bomb's fumes fed on oxygen. Therefore, the more the men inside gasped air, the faster the fumes worked to burn up their lungs. What fumes they didn't inhale were used up the same way in the air in the room.

It took about ten minutes for the excess fumes to burn up and evaporate in the air.

Carter waited that long and two more for good measure before entering.

They were dead, all five of them.

Carter strapped a sidearm, a .45, around his waist Western-style and rescued another one for Jarrell. He also gathered up three Sten guns from where they hung on the wall by their lanyards.

One of the guards sported a large ring of keys on his belt. From the size of it, Carter guessed that on it was a key for every door in the compound. He hooked the ring to his own belt and then relieved two wrists of watches.

Quickly he scurried back down the hall to Jarrell's cell.

"Sydney . . . ?"

"Ready and waiting, old man."

"Nick . . . ?"

"Coming," he told Elise. "You're next!"

The third key unlocked Jarrell's door. Jarrell popped into the hall with a wide grin on his face.

"You're a regular Houdini!"

"We'll all have to be more than that tonight," Carter replied with a smile of his own. "Can you handle these?"

"Bet your life. By the way, while you've been out and about, old man, Harley Donne arrived and went into the tunnel."

"He's the communications man?"

"The very same."

"Good. He may be the answer to the one problem I haven't been able to figure out. Load up!"

Jarrell was buckling on the .45 and slinging the Sten as Carter moved to Elise's door.

"My God, you mean we're free?" she cried, falling into his arms.

"Not by a long shot. C'mon!"

With Jarrell and Elise at his heels, Carter moved down the hall. He locked the door at the end of the hall from the inside and motioned them into the guardroom.

"Oh, my God," Elise gasped, "are they . . . ?"

"Very," Carter said, handing her one of the Sten guns.

"But how . . . ?" Jarrell began.

"Trade secret."

Carter gave Elise a thirty-second crash course on how to fire the Sten, then ushered them to a rear window.

"Here's the scene. Listen hard—I'm only telling you once. We go out through this window because the floodlights in the compound don't reach behind the building out there. We'll be in darkness and moving behind the buildings."

They both nodded their understanding, and Carter continued.

"Once outside, we hit the armory, the maintenance shed, and search for a portable generator. I'm sure they have one for emergencies. Got that?"

"Yes."

"Right-o," Jarrell nodded.

"Good. When we're set I'll brief you on the rest of it."

He handed Jarrell one of the watches he had filched from the guards.

"Ready?" Carter asked, sliding the window open.

"As I'll ever be," Elise croaked.

"Lead on, old man!" Jarrell said.

Carter rolled out the window, thinking how much he felt like the leader of the Charge of the Light Brigade and hoping the result wasn't going to be the same.

FIFTEEN

Carter parked Jarrell and Elise at the rear of a squat brick building he had already reconnoitered as the armory. From there he moved, building by building, around the compound in search of the two roaming guards.

Near the edge of the earthen mound over the tunnel, he found the spot he needed. Between the rear of the tunnel and the fence was a slanted area impossible to reach with mowers. The grass and wild flowers stood thick and nearly two feet tall.

More than enough to hide a prone man lying in wait.

From this position Carter had a clear view of the entire compound.

The two roaming guards covered their perimeters, passed under the two guard towers, and then met directly in the center of the lighted area. Here they exchanged a few words and set off again.

The whole process took twenty minutes.

Carter waited through two full rounds. Neither time, when the roaming guards met in the middle of the compound, did the two sentries in the towers pay them the slightest attention.

It was a perfect setup.

The guard patrolling the area where Carter lay had passed within five feet of him on both of his rounds.

The second guard on the opposite side moved each time into the shadows at the side of the building where Carter and the others had been held.

Carter chose that place for his attack once he had nailed the first guard.

Luckily, neither guard had Dobermans trailing along behind him.

Silently, Killmaster slid the Sten from his shoulder. He unclipped the leather lanyard from the gun's barrel and butt and wound it tightly around his hands.

The two guards finished their usual center-compound exchange and parted. As the guard approached, Carter slithered through the tall grass until he was inches from the cement retaining wall that held the mound of earth in place over the rear of the tunnel.

If the guard's pattern of patrol ran true to form, his neck would pass directly below Carter.

Nick Carter heard rather than saw the man make his turn at the front of the tunnel. Parallel to the wall was a gravel path. When Carter heard his boots hit the gravel, he tightened the muscles in his forearms and moved the lanyard forward to the very top edge of the wall.

Jarrell and Elise would be crouching in place in the shadows near the armory building. They had their instructions.

If Carter wasn't able to waste his man without a sound, they were to go into action at once with their Stens.

Objective?

Take out the second guard and the two in the towers. Once that was done they would just have to rush the tunnel and fly the rest of it by the seat of their pants.

Carter hoped that wouldn't be necessary.

The sound of boots on gravel grew louder, then suddenly stopped.

Carter's breathing stopped too, and sweat popped from every pore of his body.

Had the bastard picked this round not to go all the way to the end of the tunnel?

Seconds dragged by and became an eternity. Carter was about to chance a further slide forward for an eyeball check, when the crunching of leather on gravel resumed.

And then he saw it: the top of the man's helmet directly below him.

Carter tensed, took a deep breath, released it, and lunged.

He looped the lanyard out, down, and then yanked it back toward him.

It was a direct hit. The narrow leather strap coiled like a snake around the man's throat. Instinctively the guard's hands left his weapon and went to his throat.

Carter yanked him off his feet and slammed his shoulder blades against the cement wall. At the same time he crossed his forearms and slammed his right elbow against the back of the guard's head for leverage.

The body writhed and struggled, but with his feet inches off the ground there was no way for the guard to gain any leverage for escape.

He was going fast from lack of air, but Carter sensed not fast enough. He twisted the lanyard tighter and yanked harder. But somehow the man was able to get his thumbs between the leather and his windpipe.

When Carter heard him gasp in enough air to give a cry of alarm, he did the only thing he could do. He added the strength of his right shoulder to his forearm and leaned far forward.

One second more was all it took.

The tremendous pressure of Carter's upper body pushing the man's head forward, coupled with the guard's lower back against the wall, did its job.

His neck snapped like a dry twig.

Carter dropped instantly over the wall and went to work. He stripped the man to T-shirt and skivvies, and pulled the clothes on over his own.

Seconds later, fully dressed, Carter pulled the body farther into the shadows and checked the compound. The second guard was just moving beneath the far tower along the fence line.

He would reach the edge of their former jailhouse in about five minutes.

Carter took off across the open center of the compound. He was bathed in full light now and scanning both towers out of the corner of his eye.

Neither of the tower guards even glanced his way.

It was just about the way Carter had figured it. Their area of responsibility was outside the tall wire fence. They paid little or no attention to what went on inside.

At the front of the armory he checked the towers once more, then paused. He bent and leaned forward, careful not to throw a shadow over the door with his body.

It was double-locked: a Yale deadbolt on top and a one-tumbler German Richter on the bottom.

By the time Carter moved around the corner of the building, he had located the keys on the ring at his belt.

"Jarrell . . . ?"

"Here," came the reply, and Jarrell and Elise left the heavy grass near the edge of the fence.

"One down," Carter said, passing him the ring.

"Good show."

"Two locks," Carter whispered. "This one is for the top, this one the bottom."

"Got it."

"Cover him, Elise, when he goes in," Carter said.

"I'll try," she gulped, holding the Sten nervously in front of her.

"No, you won't," Carter snapped. "You'll *do*. If those two in the towers spot him, they'll probably come down to check rather than fire into the armory. If they start, you start . . . blasting!"

She nodded, wide-eyed, and Carter turned back to Jarrell.

"You know what to look for?"

"I do," Jarrell replied.

"Good enough."

Carter moved out at a fast but silent walk. In no time he passed the buildings between the armory and the prison building.

He came around the corner and saw the second guard near the fence, gazing out into the darkness. He stood with his back to Carter, his weight on one foot. He looked relaxed, and then Carter saw the red ember in his cupped hand and smiled.

The guard was grabbing an out-of-sight quick smoke.

The Sten lay cradled in his arm and stayed there, even though Carter made no pretense at silence as he approached.

"That you, Rafe?"

Carter growled a muffled "Yeah" and let part of his khaki-covered shoulder and his helmet fall into a shaft of light.

Carter moved up swiftly behind him, slipping the heavy, standard issue .45 from the leather at his hip. He flipped it in his hand until the smooth barrel creased his palm.

"You fer a bloody smoke too, huh, mate? Bloody stupid rule . . ."

He never finished the sentence.

Carter swung the automatic as hard as he could. The heavy butt struck the guard in the side of the neck. The dull thud of steel against flesh was louder than Carter had expected, but it was still not loud enough to sound an alarm.

The man uttered an odd sound that was a cross between a gasp and a moan as he stumbled, then fell to his knees.

Carter stepped around him, pulling his head up by the front of his helmet. He flipped the .45 in his hand and struck again with equal force, laying the barrel across the guard's windpipe.

This time there was no sound beyond the dull thud of the body hitting the soft earth.

Just as he had the first guard, Carter stripped this one. When he had the clothes bundled, he slipped through the shadows back to the dark side of the armory.

"Is he in?" Carter asked, sliding into a crouch beside Elise.

"Yes. I heard the rear window open."

Carter nodded in the darkness and moved around the corner to the rear of the building.

"Jarrell . . . ?"

"I'm right here . . . at the window."

Carter removed the guard's lighter from the bundle of clothes and slid his hand between the bars.

"There's a lighter."

"Got it."

"Be careful how you wave it around in there! Clothes coming through."

Carter shoved the boots between the bars of the window and then the clothing, one garment at a time.

He heard Jarrell dressing and then saw the flame of the lighter.

"Stay away from the front windows, and shield the light as much as you can."

"Will do, old chap."

Carter heard him move away, and then he settled down to wait, forcing his taut muscles to relax.

It seemed like the better part of an hour, but Carter knew it was less than five minutes before Jarrell was back.

"Found the stuff," he hissed. "You sure four will be enough?"

"Just enough."

"Then here they are!"

Carter found the other man's hands in the darkness and relieved them of the four fist-sized balls of plastique explosive.

"Got 'em," he said. "Detonators?"

"Coming through, and the lighter."

Carter added the detonators to the balls of plastique in his arms and moved back around the building to join Elise.

"All right?" she asked.

"Fine. How're you doing?"

"I'm scared to death."

"Good," Carter said. "Fear will keep you on your toes."

"He's coming out!"

"I hear," Carter said, clicking off the safety on his Sten. "You take the tower on the left."

Sweat dripped into Carter's eyes as he heard the door of the armory open and then close. The guard in the right-hand tower turned and moved to the inside rail.

Carter flattened himself and raised the muzzle of the Sten until the gun's forward sights were dead on the center of the man's chest.

Jarrell stepped into the light, fully dressed as a guard now, with the Sten slung at his shoulder.

Over the sight Carter saw the tower guard's eyes squint and his features twist into a mask of puzzlement.

Carter was about to squeeze off a burst, when Jarrell came through. He lifted his right arm and gave the tower sentry a jaunty wave.

The man's face relaxed. He returned the wave and moved back to the outside rail of the tower.

"Whew," came the sound of expelled air from Elise's lips.

"I agree . . . whew," Carter said as Jarrell passed into the darkness behind the building. "Come on!"

With Elise at his heels, Carter moved behind the armory to the building he had already made as the maintenance shack.

The window was unbarred but locked from the inside.

Quickly he removed his shirt and wrapped it around the butt of the .45. One tap cracked a pane. A second one split it enough so that Carter could carefully pick out the pieces.

In no time the window was open and Carter had passed Elise the lighter.

"You know what to look for?"

"Yes, the emergency generator."

"Right. Up you go!"

She was agile as a cat. One lift and she was through the window and dropping on the inside.

While Carter waited, he shrugged back into the shirt and straightened his uniform. He also stored the plastique and the detonators in any pockets he could find.

"Nick . . . ?"

"Yeah?"

"You were right. It's here, just as you described it."

"Good. Did you find the automatic switch?"

"I think so, under a plastic cover. There are four different-colored wires leading into what looks like a little steel plate."

"That's it," Carter said, keeping the elation in his voice to a minimum. "When the outside power goes off, that plate will be tripped. It will interface with another just like it. That starts the generator. You know when to pull the plate back and kill it?"

"Yes," came the quaking reply.

"See you in the tunnel," Carter said and, without waiting for a reply, moved off.

He followed the fence line all the way around to the rear of the tunnel where he had left the first guard. Jarrell started his walk across the center of the compound seconds later.

Carter waited until he was sure they would meet dead center and then stepped out.

The timing was perfect, and they got no more than a single, cursory glance from one of the tower guards.

Just as they came together, Carter turned in a three-quarter stance away from the towers. Jarrell did the same, with his shoulder touching Carter's.

"Generator?"

"She got it," Carter said. "Two for you, two for me."

He passed across the two balls of plastique and two of the detonators. The whole quickly disappeared into Jarrell's pockets.

"Nine minutes on one. Ten minutes and thirty seconds on the other."

"Right," Jarrell said. "Time?"

Carter scanned his wrist and waited until the watch's second hand was precisely on twelve.

"Two-o-five . . . sharp."

"Check," Jarrell nodded. "Good luck."

"No luck involved, my friend, just timing . . . very precise timing."

The two men parted, moving their separate ways across the clearing. Carter had barely passed into the darkness beside the tunnel when he broke into a light jog. He skirted the rear of the tunnel, found the fence, and veered right.

Twice he slowed to a measured walk as he passed through paths of light. Beyond them he jogged again until he was at the corner of the compound and the base of a tall utility pole.

Above him, midway up the pole, he could see the outline of the fat transformer box. Above it, barely visible, were the incoming power lines.

Carter worked one roll of plastique around the base of the pole and then pulled a detonator from his pocket.

The dial was almost impossible to see in the darkness, and Carter cursed. Cautiously he moved toward the light, stopping when there was enough illumination to read his watch and the face of the detonator.

". . . five . . . four . . . three . . . two . . . one . . . set."

The clicking of the timer was like a miniature ratchet. When the hand read ten minutes thirty seconds, he scurried back to the pole and jammed the hot-point into the doughy plastique.

When he was sure it was secure, Carter moved along the fence line toward the guard tower on his side of the compound.

As he walked he set the second detonator at nine minutes and readied the second ball of plastique in his other hand.

Twenty yards from the tower he looked up. The sentry was on the opposite side. Carter could see only his boots and a few inches of his khaki uniform pants.

When he was right beside the tower, he darted beneath it. He found the center of the X-cross brace that anchored the tower's four legs and mashed the plastique over it. In almost the same motion he jammed the detonator in the center of the gray explosive and moved back into the light.

Following the pattern of the real guards, he paced to the main gate and then back across the front of the tunnel. The huge steel door was closed and the peephole showed no light.

He made the turn, moved into the darkness, and immediately stopped. Then he crouched and, for the first time since setting the charges, grabbed a look at the watch on his wrist.

Three minutes to go.

Figuring a two-minute walk to the center of the clearing, he searched the other side of the compound for Jarrell.

And then he saw him, coming around the end of the building that had held them, a wide smile on his face.

". . . four . . . three . . . two . . . one . . . bang."

They stood in the center of the clearing, lanyards loosened and safeties off on the Stens.

Both men held their breaths for three more long seconds before the night actually exploded.

Jarrell's tower went first. The plastique made kindling out of the legs and cross braces, and it came down in a heap. The sentry's loud scream amid the rubble preceded the second blast by two seconds.

Somehow the sentry in the second tower survived the blast and the fall. He came toward them out of the rubble, staggering and waving his arms.

A shaft of light knifed toward them from the peephole in the tunnel's steel door. Whoever was behind it, peering out, saw the two sentries in the center of the yard standing perplexed with their Stens at the ready. They were obviously ready to fire, but there was nothing to fire at.

"Shall I drop him?" Jarrell hissed.

"Not yet. Let's hope they still think it's some kind of an accident. If we fire before the blackout, they might not panic."

"C'mon," Jarrell growled under his breath, "blow, damnit, blow!"

As if his words were guiding the other two detonators,

the plastique at the base of the power poles went off at the same time.

The entire compound blacked out and seconds later everything was silent.

In the darkness, Carter and Jarrell moved cautiously toward the stairs of the tunnel.

In his mind, Carter tried to match the thoughts of those three men on the other side of the steel door.

An accident in the armory? . . . Where are the other guards? . . . Why has the power failed? . . . And when it did, why hasn't the emergency generator kicked on?

The stillness was nerve-shattering, and the wait seemed as if it would go on forever.

And then—probably because of the dead silence—the men in the tunnel made their decision.

Carter heard the bolts being thrown back. Then the door thudded open. When he heard the unmistakable sound of boots on the concrete steps, he turned his head slightly toward the line of buildings far to his left and shouted at the top of his lungs.

"Elise!"

There was a chugging sound, then a whir that grew steadily louder, and then light flooded the tunnel and speared toward them through the open door.

Two men stood at the top of the stairs, Sten guns held carelessly across their chests. With the backlighting they made perfect targets.

Carter stitched both of them with a long, figure-eight blast from his own Sten and heard Jarrell's gun chatter from his side.

"Get him!" Carter shouted, already coming to his feet. "Let's go!"

Jarrell had felled the last guard from the towers. Carter had dropped two of the three they knew were in the tunnel. That left Lenore Grayburn, Harley Donne, and one unknown man.

They took the stairs in one leap and rolled through the doorway side by side. Once through, Carter veered to the left, Jarrell to the right.

Their man was about thirty yards away, wildly spinning the dials of a console before him.

When he saw them, his right hand clawed a .45 from the holster at his hip.

Carter and Jarrell fired as one on the way down. The man screamed in agony as one or both of the bursts cut his legs out from beneath him.

He hit the floor with a sickening thud, but he was still game enough to make one more try with the automatic.

He got off a single shot as Carter sprayed a burst of 9mm slugs four inches off the floor in his direction.

The .45 hit the tiles as the body twitched a couple of times and then lay still.

Both men were on their feet at the same time, charging down each side of the aisle.

"You take the right-hand door, I'll take the left," Carter shouted. "And watch yourself!"

He kicked the first door open, sprayed the interior, and rolled in.

Empty.

He heard Jarrell do the same on the other side of the hall.

They worked their way down the hall until only two doors remained: one left, one right.

Carter knew the one on the right to be the office where he had been interrogated by Lenore Grayburn.

"This one first," he whispered, crouching by the right-hand door.

"Me first," Jarrell hissed, already coiling in front of the door. "I hope she's waiting."

Carter started to call out to him, when the door behind them slowly began to open.

The next few seconds seemed to go by in slow motion.

Carter levered his Sten around to cover the opening door.

Jarrell lunged against the office door, sending it inward with his body right behind it.

Harley Donne, his face ashen, his eyes behind his

glasses as large as saucers, stepped through the door. His hands were far above his head, and tears were running like twin rivers down his cheeks.

"Lie down . . . flat and spread!" Carter hissed.

The words were barely out of his mouth when the interior of Lenore Grayburn's office exploded.

The blast hit Carter in the back of the head and neck like a sledgehammer.

He saw the opposite wall come up to meet him, and then he was rolling, spiraling down a long tunnel toward total blackness.

SIXTEEN

"Nick . . . Nick . . . Nick . . ."

There was a swelling tide of water right in front of his eyes the first two times he tried to blink them open. On the third try the tide seemed to recede. In its place he saw Elise Pearson's beautiful face swirling above his own.

"Nick . . ."

"Yeah . . . I'm still among the living."

He tried to move his head from her soft lap and sit up. With the first moves the aches and pains in every part of his battered body asserted themselves.

"Ohhh . . ."

"Go easy," she said, her voice sounding to Carter's ears as if it were coming from a deep well. "I don't think there are any bones broken, but you've got tiny cuts all over your back and legs."

"Help me up."

She did, in sections, until he was finally swaying on his feet.

Beyond Elise he saw Harley Donne squatting Buddha-like against the far wall. "How long has he been like that?" Carter asked, pointing.

"Since I came in. He said 'Don't shoot' four or five times. That's it."

"He hasn't been near a radio?"

"No. He hasn't moved."

"Where's Jarrell?"

Now it was Elise's turn to sway a little. "He . . . he's in there . . ."

Just from the look on her face and the tone of her voice, Carter knew that Sydney Jarrell was dead. Nevertheless, he staggered across the hall and into what was left of Lenore Grayburn's office to see for himself.

The room was a mess.

It could have been plastique, but more than likely it was a couple of high-impact grenades.

There wasn't much left of Jarrell or Lenore Grayburn. Just enough to tell that one of them had been a man and the other a woman.

She must have been waiting just inside the door with her thumbs on the firing pins, hoping to get both of them. And she probably would have if Jarrell's body hadn't partially shielded Carter from the blast.

Yessiree, he thought, *no doubt about it.* Lenore Grayburn was a radical to the last.

Carter swayed back into the hall.

"He was a good man."

Elise only nodded.

Carter searched the floor until he found the .45 that had been lifted from the holster at his side.

When he found it, he moved to Harley Donne and ground the gun's muzzle into the man's ear.

"Don't . . . Oh, dear God, man, don't!"

"See that wall over there, Harley?"

"Yes . . . yes . . . oh, God . . ."

"I want you to answer a lot of questions very carefully and do a lot of things very quickly . . ."

"Yes . . . yes!"

"And if you don't, Harley, I'm going to paint that wall with your brains. Do you understand, Harley?"

"Yes . . . I'll do anything. I didn't want all of this . . . I was blackmailed . . ."

"I don't give a damn about your reasons, Harley; that's in the past. It's the future that counts now. Move!"

The little man moved without any further prodding from the .45. He moved so fast, in fact, that Carter had to force his weary body to keep up.

In the main part of the tunnel, Carter steered him toward the largest and most impressive-looking of the consoles.

"Sit! You know how to operate this?"

"Yes. I set it all up."

Nick Carter gave the little communications expert crisp, clear directions and watched him closely. He was no expert himself at computer-run satellite communications, but he did know enough to monitor Harley Donne's actions.

The business end of the ugly .45 still pressed against Harley's quivering neck also bought insurance that the little man would do what he was told without deviation.

Carter gave him the bypass codes to get the Washington special lines and then the correct sequence to push the "Urgent" message on through to Dupont Circle.

While they were waiting for the relays to take effect, Carter fired questions at the other man.

They were answered as fast as they were asked.

"Yes," Harley jabbered, "it works close to that. Admiral Hamilton will run base command out of the house in Maine. One entire floor has been renovated over to a COMSAT similar to this one."

"Good grief," Elise mumbled from behind Carter. "No wonder my husband didn't want me near the Maine house."

"And this place," Carter said. "This is to be prime secondary and backup?"

Harley Donne nodded and droplets of sweat flew from his face.

"Right, plus this was to be European command center under Lady Grayburn."

"Who gives the final word?" Carter rasped.

"Admiral Hamilton in Maine. Once the *Shark*'s missiles are in the air, I jam all satellite frequencies from here. Except one, that is. When that happens, the admiral will inform all the NATO and Western allied nations of what is happening."

Carter cursed and chewed his lip for a moment, his

mind whirling with the ramifications of what Donne was telling him.

"So they won't have much of a choice. Either fire first or swallow the Soviet retaliation of the *Shark*'s missiles."

Harley Donne nodded, swallowed, and looked as if he was going to be sick.

A familiar voice came up on the large speakers above Carter's head. Carter grabbed a short-stand mike and slipped into a chair beside Donne at the console. After a verbal code exchange that let Hawk know that it was indeed his top agent on the London end, Carter began filling his boss in on the situation.

When he had finished, Carter could almost hear the gears of the other man's trip-hammer mind working.

"We already have a team ready in Japan. Now that we have an exact location of the *Shark*, it should be fairly easy to take them."

"Yeah," Carter replied, "as long as Owen Hamilton doesn't give thc 'fire' order while they're moving in!"

"Then we'll have to take the Maine house first. Are you sure no one at the base there warned Hamilton that you'd taken over?"

Carter turned to Harley.

"No . . . I'm sure. There wasn't time," the little man said.

As if to prove it, he showed Carter the constant signal that was being sent from the station where they sat to the U.S.

"We're sure," Carter growled to Hawk.

"Is the Pearson woman there with you?"

"Yes."

"Ask her if there is any way we can get into the Maine house without a direct frontal attack."

Carter turned to Elise. "You heard him."

"Yes," she replied, screwing her brows into a frown. "There is a way. Or, at least, there was once, a long time ago."

"Explain," Carter said, urgency in his voice.

"The original house was just three rooms. It was built just after the Revolutionary War by a smuggler. There are tunnels from the beach up to that part of the house. But . . ."

"But what?"

"My father and I found them when I was a little girl. I . . . I can't remember exactly where the openings are."

Carter thought for a moment, then grabbed her arm in a viselike grip. "Could you find them if you were there?"

"Yes . . . I think so."

Carter spun back to the microphone. It was a long shot, but a workable play had already formed in his mind. He relayed it to Hawk.

"It might work," Hawk replied.

"It has to work. Do you have a positive vetting on anyone high up in British SIS?"

"Definitely."

"Good," Carter replied. "Get him, and have him put the best possible team together to hold this place down here. I think it's best to go to the top. It's hard to say who else in MI5 or Special Branch Hamilton has turned."

"I'll get right on it," Hawk said.

"And have a Harrier here as soon as possible." Carter paused and checked his watch. "It's three in the morning our time. If we scramble fast we can be out of here by four."

"I'll make the fastest thing we've got over there available," Hawk said. "You can be in Maine by two A.M. our time."

Nick Carter smiled.

Two o'clock in the morning in Maine would still be nice and dark.

"I'll have a commando team our best waiting here."

Carter rattled off the gear he and Elise would need, and then closed out.

"I had a couple of very dear friends when I checked in

here, Harley . . ." The little man looked to Elise. "No, Harley, I mean a stiletto and a 9mm Luger."

"If Lady Grayburn had them, they would be somewhere in her desk."

Carter turned to Elise. "Watch him. If one finger touches a dial, cut him in half."

Elise gulped but nodded resolutely. Carter had no doubt she would do it if she had to.

Carter, rejuvenated now, moved quickly down the hall and into what was left of Lady Grayburn's office. Ignoring the human carnage, he went directly to the desk.

It took him almost fifteen minutes to throw the rubble away and get to the desk proper. In no time he had the drawers open.

Besides Hugo and Wilhelmina, he found an impressive-looking leather folder. In it were jumbled words and letters, as well as country and rank designations beside them.

Back in the CommCenter room, he dropped the folder in front of Harley Donne.

"My guess is that this is the worldwide membership of JOUST."

"I . . . I don't know," Harley replied. "I've never seen it before."

"Do you have a letter-number code designation?"

"Yes."

"What is it?"

The little man rattled off a series of letter-numbers, and Carter went to work.

In less than two minutes he had found Harley in the book.

The discovery brought a smile to Carter's face.

He wasn't an expert on cryptography, but there were people at AXE who were.

Carter guessed that within hours they could crack the codes in the book, and Hawk could start dropping a net over JOUST around the world.

The sound of a jet engine sent him running to the tunnel entrance.

A vertical-landing British Harrier was just setting down in the center of the clearing.

SEVENTEEN

Nick Carter checked the waterproof chronometer on his wrist. It was 3:31 in the U.S.A., Eastern Standard Time.

"I'm ready."

"Yes, you are," was all Carter could say.

The black second skin of the wet suit hugged Elise's generous curves, making her wondrous body even more wondrous. Her hair had been stuffed under a black skullcap that melded with the suit at her neck. Her white face gleamed contrastingly against the suit.

"Something wrong?"

"Only your makeup."

"My makeup?" she exclaimed, her hands going to her face. "I don't have any on . . ."

"I know," Carter said, lifting a small jar from the bunk beside him and uncapping it.

She peered inside the jar and made a face. "God, what's that?"

"The best thing to call it is black goo," Carter said with a laugh, dipping a generous gob onto his fingers and handing the jar to her. "Cover your face completely. It dries fast and hard."

She wrinkled her nose in obvious distaste but did as she was told.

Minutes later they stood in front of the cabin mirror side by side, black from head to toe.

Carter was armed to the teeth. A silenced Wilhelmina was holstered at his right hip in a watertight zip sheath. Hugo was strapped outside the wet suit to his right leg, and a larger, Fairboron-Sykes commando knife was on the left side of the belt.

A waterproof pouch containing four grenades and a handful of flash blinders, as well as two wads of plastique and spare magazines, hung from the back of his belt.

As a heavy piece, there was a 9mm Uzi submachine gun strapped over his right shoulder. The metal butt had been removed so that the deadly little piece was only about nine pounds with a fully loaded forty-round magazine and about seventeen inches long.

"Looking at you, I feel naked," Elise commented wryly.

"Don't," Carter replied gruffly. "You don't need to be armed. You're not going all the way in, remember?"

She was about to reply, but Captain Arnold Weston stepped into the tiny cabin.

He had an earnest, fleshy face partially covered by a ginger-colored beard. His stocky body was covered by black jeans and a turtleneck sweater.

All in all, he looked like what he was: a salty old New England fisherman.

"Your gear is ready topside. We're exactly off La-Croix Point, about five miles out."

"Thank you, Captain. How's the sea?"

"Running heavy on the surface," he replied, "but with the sled you can go deep enough so it won't bother you."

"Good enough," Carter said, turning to Elise. "Ready?"

"As I'll ever be."

"Good. Let's go."

The house sat on a rise in rough, rocky terrain about a hundred and fifty yards in from the sea. The fenced shoreline was about a mile long, and almost nowhere could a boat land in calm seas, let alone if the waves were choppy.

The underwater sled was the only way they would be able to get deep into the rocks without detection. And even that would be hazardous.

"You've used one of these?" Captain Weston asked as his two crewmen lowered the sled over the seaward side of the fishing trawler.

"Several times," Carter said, giving Elise a hand over

the side to the ladder that led down to the roiling sea.

"Good. Your depth and distance gauge lights are shielded, but you'd better snap them off just the same when you near the surface."

"Will do," Carter said, swinging over the side and dropping into the water.

"Good hunting," the captain said, bringing two fingers to his forehead.

Carter gave him the same salute, then activated the sled's small twin props. They started to move at once.

"You hang on here. I'll control the rudders. Keep your hip touching mine so our bodies shift together as close as possible. Got it?"

"Nothing to it. Nick . . . ?"

"Yeah?"

"What if Hamilton gives the signal to the *Shark* to fire before you get to him?"

Carter's lips set in a grim line. "We just hope they're monitoring the right channel in Japan and move in fast enough."

"And if they don't?"

"We'll never know it."

Carter pushed the throttle forward, and they began to move. When he had cleared the fishing boat, he bent the rudder handle and they disappeared into the sea.

A hundred yards out, Carter killed the gauge lights and brought the sled to the surface. When he broke into the air, he throttled back and killed the power.

"How're we lookin'?" he whispered to Elise beside him.

"We're a little up coast, but not enough to cause a problem."

It was a cloudy, overcast night, but there was enough gray light sifting through the clouds to see and be seen.

Carter cased the rocky shoreline through narrowed eyes. He didn't see a sentry, but he knew they were there, somewhere.

"Can you take us in from here?"

"I'm sure of it," she answered.

"Okay. Drop your tank!"

Carter struggled out of his own tank and then ruptured the pontoons on the sled. In seconds the small craft slithered away beneath them toward the sea bottom.

Using just his hands for communication now, he motioned Elise forward.

They covered eighty of the hundred or so yards in no time, partially on the surface but mostly submerged.

The last twenty yards were the hairy ones, but Elise seemed to know the tide. She led them skillfully into a channel between jagged rocks until they were bouncing easily in an eddy about twenty yards inland.

"This way!" she whispered.

Somehow she found footing among the rocks that quickly turned into a tide-worn path. Together, like two black specters, they blended into and moved through the worn boulders.

In another twenty yards the rocks evened out to a steady rise. Carter called a halt by tapping her on the shoulder.

"Sneakers!" he whispered.

They both removed the rubber flippers from their feet and slid on sneakers.

"Give me the layout."

Elise leaned close to his ear. "We're directly below the house, about ninety yards out. Just above us . . . there . . . the rocks give out and the gardens start."

"So if there are any guards, that's where they'll be."

"Probably. The footing down here is treacherous unless you know where you're going."

"Okay, now the big question."

"The tunnel openings?" Carter nodded. "There are two, one left, one right. The tide is in, so the one to the left is out. We'd be drowned before we got to the end."

"And ten-to-one that's the easiest entrance to find, right?"

"Yes, damnit, it is. But I think I can still find the other one at night."

"Then lead on!"

Carter stayed right on Elise's heels, and it was no easy

task. Obviously she had spent one hell of a lot of time scampering over these rocks. That, plus her natural athletic agility, left Carter scrambling more than once.

Then suddenly she came to a halt.

"We're very near the fence line here . . . not more than twenty yards."

"And the entrance?"

"Up there somewhere . . . just where the heavy undergrowth starts."

Carter didn't like the look of it. Coming up over the rocks they would be outlined for several seconds against the gray sky.

"Is there any way up—instead of over the rim of the rocks—where we would be less conspicuous?"

"The fence line."

"Move!"

There was a well-worn path along the fence line all the way up. They were nearly at the top moving in a painful crouch, when the sound of a human cough froze them both in their tracks.

Carter motioned Elise back and dropped to his belly. Like a snake he slithered the last few feet and then, cautiously, moved just his eyes over the rocky rise.

He stood on the rocks about twenty yards away from Carter, an M-16 slug over his left shoulder. He was in green fatigues, complete with helmet and combat boots.

The huge old summer house was outlined against the sky behind him. In the distance, down the rocky shoreline, Carter counted four more sentries standing, gazing out to sea.

All of them looked alert as hell.

Piercing the grayness near the house, Carter counted several more moving through the gloom. The roof was no better. He spotted at least five moving from chimney to chimney.

Soundlessly he slid back down to where Elise waited. He motioned her back until he was sure they were out of hearing range.

"No way," he whispered. "They're crawling all over the place up there!"

To Carter's surprise, he saw Elise's perfect white teeth flash in her blackened face. It could have only been a smile.

"It's all right," she said.

"How so?"

"I've got my bearings. The tunnel opening is right there!"

Carter followed her pointing finger to a spot they had already passed about twenty yards back.

As one, they moved.

Using the Fairboron-Sykes, Carter worked carefully at the rocks, hoping that the sound of the sea would drown out the scraping of the knife.

A half hour later, he had removed enough rock to make a hole large enough to crawl through.

Once inside, he helped Elise through and she led them by memory and feel.

"We're far enough in now, with two turns behind us. You can use your light."

Carter fished the penlight from beneath his belt and snapped it on.

"My God, it goes on forever . . ."

"Only as far as the wine cellar."

They moved quickly now. This deep in the earth, sound made little difference.

A fast jog and four turns brought them to a rotting ladder that led straight up.

"At the top is the trapdoor I told you about. It opens onto a crawlspace that goes only one way. At the end of it is the back side of a wine rack. The release catch is above the upper left-hand corner."

"Okay. You've got the flare gun?"

"Yes."

"See you in one hour."

"You'd better!"

Carter planted a quick kiss on her parted lips and started

up the ladder, desperately hoping that no one in the house had a late-night craving for a bottle of wine.

The wine rack door had protested loudly when Carter pushed it open enough to slip through.

Beyond it, thankfully, there had been only silence and a scampering rat or two.

Now he made his way through the old cellars, going over the layout of the rooms above in Elise's own words.

"The master suite is the tower room in the left wing of the house facing the sea. I should imagine Admiral Hamilton would be using that suite.

"There are back stairs going up from the kitchen to that wing. From the master suite there are private stairs down to the bar/den. My father had them built. The bar/den is adjacent to the great room. That must be where they have set up the equipment. It's the only room large enough."

The final stairs led up to a trapdoor that opened into one corner of the kitchen.

Carter eased it up just enough to see a man in a naval ensign's uniform at a table in the center of the room. He was munching on a sandwich and sipping a bottle of beer.

Carter dropped the door and moved back down the stairs. With the aid of his penlight and a wine sack, he managed to corral one of the rats he had seen previously.

When Carter lifted the trapdoor a second time, the man was standing at the refrigerator with his back to him. Carter put the open mouth of the sack through the opening, and the rat ran for daylight.

Any man, no matter how brave, can be taken unawares by a squeaking rat.

This one was no different.

With his back still to Carter, he put the table between himself and the rodent. So intent was he on watching the furry little creature, he never heard the trap open and the sneakered feet on the tiled floor.

Carter pulled the two feet of piano wire from the chronometer as he moved.

The ensign's gaze was still on the rat as the wire wrapped around his neck and life left his body.

Carter unceremoniously dumped him down the trap, then found the rear stairs.

At the top, it wasn't too difficult to spot the door that led to the master suite. Two fatigue-clad guards were standing at rigid attention on each side of it.

Carter unsheathed Wilhelmina and started firing just as he hit the top of the stairs.

He head-shot one and pumped two into the chest of the other.

There was no sound other than the dull thud of their bodies hitting the carpeted floor.

AXE's Killmaster didn't pause even half a step. He walked right over them and went through the door, slamming it behind him.

"Yes . . . what . . . ?"

Hamilton was in shirt sleeves, sitting at a desk.

He took one look at Carter's wet suit and blackened face, and dived for the bedside stand.

Carter's gaze followed his path of flight. When he was sure of Hamilton's intent, he squeezed Wilhelmina's trigger.

The slug caught him high, just above the right shoulder blade, and flattened him.

Before he could recover, Carter stepped over him and snatched a black plastic box from the bedside stand. A small red bulb glowed on the top of the box, and just below it was a red button.

Carter had few doubts about the red button.

"Carter . . ." Hamilton gasped, recognizing him now through the black goo at closer range.

Carter nodded and leaned over the man, placing the Luger's muzzle at his temple.

"You can save the lives of your men if you go downstairs with me right now and tell them to lay down their arms."

"Go to hell."

The 9mm slug entered Admiral Owen Hamilton's head

just above his left ear. The right side of his head exploded somewhere under the bed.

Carter found the wall switch and blinked the lights of the master suite three times.

He had exactly five minutes before Elise fired the flare gun.

At the foot of the stairs, Carter quickly moved across the den. One of two large double doors stood open.

There were three men in the living room that had now been converted into a war room. One stood at a table, pouring himself a cup of coffee. Two others were sitting at consoles, smoking and talking.

Carter took the two at the consoles out first, then walked into the room.

"What the . . . ?"

Two steel-jacketed slugs tore through the man's chest. The coffee cup went straight into the air, and his body sailed backward over the table.

Carter stuck Wilhelmina in his belt and cranked up the Uzi as he closed the room's three doors and locked them from the inside.

He then found a transmitter that was hot but not locked to a certain frequency. Quickly he spun the dial, locked it in, and began to tap the "Send" key.

The answer was immediate.

Rapidly he tapped out two longs, a short, and then three longs.

From somewhere in the bowels of Washington, the same message—"Go"—would be flashed to Japan.

At that instant, Carter saw a flash of white soar through the night sky outside the window.

Within seconds, the Maine night was turned into day. Searchlights were everywhere, and in the distance Carter could hear helicopters.

From the window he saw grenades rip huge holes in the tall wire fence. Another ear-crunching explosion told him that the front gate had ceased to exist.

Shouting at one of the living room doors made Carter

turn and bring up the Uzi.

By the time the door gave, Killmaster was ready.

About eight of them rolled into the room. The forty rounds from the Uzi cut all but two of them in half.

A grenade caught those two halfway down the stairs.

Suddenly the house, inside, was quiet. There was still some firing and a lot of shouting outside, but Carter paid it very little attention.

He moved back to the console and lit a cigarette to wait.

Fifteen minutes later, the Morse signal came through:

140-40 CLEAR AND SECURE. YOU?

Carter tapped the key:

HERE TOO

"Mr. Carter?"

Carter looked up. A tall U.S. Marine in full battle dress stood in the doorway.

"Yes, I'm Carter."

"The area is secure, sir."

"And the woman?"

"Safe, sir."

"Good. I'll be right down."

Carter smiled and lit another cigarette as he moved toward the door, the stairs, and hopefully, to Elise Pearson.

DON'T MISS THE NEXT NEW NICK CARTER SPY THRILLER

DEATH ISLAND

They were given a room on the top floor front with two large double beds, a huge ceiling fan, and a wonderful view of the park, the beach and the pleasure boat docks. A cool breeze came in off the ocean, and Carter stripped down to his shorts and went out onto the balcony.

Tieggs's nostrils flared slightly at the sight of Carter's Luger and his razor sharp stiletto but he said nothing.

Carter picked up the phone but before he rang for room service he turned back to Tieggs. "Get back out to my room at the base and grab my tuxedo and formal pumps. Get yourself a suit of clothes and get back here."

"I don't understand."

"We're going to the governor's party."

"But we haven't been invited."

Carter laughed as he dialed. "We're going to crash the party. I wouldn't want to miss the governor's wife for anything in the world."

"Gabrielle," Tieggs said softly.

"Yes, Gabrielle. Now get going." The hotel room service clerk answered. "This is Carter in 301. Bring me a bottle of your best dark rum, a pitcher of papaya juice, and some ice."

"Immediately, *monsieur,*" the clerk said, and when Carter hung up and looked around, Tieggs was gone.

He got up, went back into the room, and opened the door so that he could look out into the corridor. It was dimly lit and deserted. There was absolutely no noise in the hotel. The building could have been deserted.

He softly closed the door, lit himself a cigarette, then got his Luger. He took his silencer from his trouser pocket, screwed it on the end of the barrel, then pulled out several bills and laid them on the bureau. He went back out onto the balcony and sat down, his feet up on the low table.

Room service in the person of a very young Chinese boy showed up ten minutes later with his rum, juice, and ice, and Carter paid his tip, and mixed himself a large drink.

Back out on the balcony, the room lights out, he sat back, the Luger on the chair beside him, and slowly sipped his drink as he watched the occasional car or passerby below on the street and in the park.

The town was very quiet at this time of the night. But Carter suspected that was not normally the case. He supposed that what action there might normally be here in town was tonight centered up at the governor's mansion.

Contrary to what Tieggs thought, Carter suspected that Governor Rondine was somehow involved in the tracking site's problems. His motives were so patently obvious that the previous investigators had given the man the benefit of the doubt. Carter was not so inclined.

It was nearing nine o'clock when Carter heard a slight noise at the door. He picked up the Luger and slipped the safety to the off position, then held the gun high against his chest. His back was to the door, but whoever was coming in from the corridor would present a silhouette target.

He waited a full three seconds, then spun off the chair to the left, bringing his Luger up into a firing position. But if the door was open, then whoever had come in had first switched off the corridor lights, because there was nothing to the other side of the room but a vague darkness.

A flash of light and the whine of a bullet ricocheting off

the balcony railing just above Carter came a moment later. Carter fired three shots in quick succession, one where the light flash had been and one on either side of it, then flattened himself on the deck and waited.

A soft scraping noise came to him from the left, near the bed, but he resisted the urge to fire.

A truck rumbled by on the street below, turned the corner, beeped its horn and then was gone.

A signal? Carter rolled to the right back toward where he had been sitting a split instant before a powerful flashlight was switched on and two shots were fired at that very spot.

—From DEATH ISLAND
A New Nick Carter Spy Thriller
From Charter in May